TALES OF THE DARK FEMININE

Inspirational Stories of the World's Fiercest Goddesses

V. Castro

TALES OF THE DARK FEMININE

Inspirational Stories of the World's Fiercest Goddesses

WATKINS

Tales of the Dark Feminine
by V Castro

This edition first published in the UK and USA in 2025 by
Watkins, an imprint of Watkins Media Limited
Unit 11, Shepperton House, 89-93 Shepperton Road
London, N1 3DF

enquiries@watkinspublishing.com

2 3 4 5 6 7 8 9 10

Designed and typeset by JCS Publishing Services Ltd
Printed and bound by CPI Group (UK) Ltd, Croydon, CR0 4YY

Design: Alice Claire Coleman
Illustrations: Sally Taylor
Commissioning Editor: Fiona Robertson
Managing Editor: Daniel Culver
Project Editor: Gigi St John
Production: Uzma Taj

The manufacturer's authorised representative in the EU for product safety is:
eucomply OÜ - Pärnu mnt 139b-14, 11317 Tallinn, Estonia,
hello@eucompliancepartner.com, www.eucompliancepartner.com

A CIP record for this book is available from the British Library

ISBN: 978-1-78678-998-3 (Hardback)
ISBN: 978-1-83681-018-6 (eBook)

www.watkinspublishing.com

MIX
Paper | Supporting responsible forestry
FSC® C013604

Contents

Introduction

Today, the dark feminine is a vibe. Goddess energy is celebrated across popular culture and social media, but what was it before it became a buzzword? It's true the gods of mythology and creatures of folklore desired followers, devotees and offerings, but our modern lives hardly resemble those of the original believers, for whom these beings were the creators of what we now see as natural phenomena. We have data and science to explain away the things once thought mystical or malevolent. But our primal emotions, our fears and desires, are the same as those of the first people who sat around a fire and told a story in the dark. What can we learn by going back in time to revisit the stories of fierce feminine archetypes? Even the ones we now label as horrifying can teach us something. The dark feminine is more than just a sultry aesthetic.

The dark – your shadow self – is as valuable as the light. The dark feminine knows to her core who she is. If there isn't a seat at the table for you, then you create your own table with head held high. Your individuality trumps pleasing others or chasing dopamine hits from clickbait. How you look, who you know, what you earn, your follower count – none of those things matters. Real dark femininity doesn't waste time judging or putting others down for self-validation.

The dark feminine has gone through some shit and wears that as a badge of honour. She doesn't follow the pack or ask for permission to be who she is. She is the dark and the flame in the dark. She knows that she has a purpose.

Dark goddess energy speaks for itself. It is focused, yet untamed in its desire to accomplish the task at hand. The dark feminine never plays the victim and always speaks the truth as if the tongue were a sword. The Egyptian goddess Isis believed in her power so much, she went on a quest to raise the dead.

One thing I like about these goddess tales is their emphasis that perfect does not exist. Goddesses have faults and can stumble on their own egos, but they also know when and how to wield their power. The Greek goddess Athena is renowned for her warrior power and artistic skills, yet in her story she allowed the boasting of a mortal girl to get the better of her and in her desire to be the best she caused tragedy. The Hindu deity Kali, the great destroyer, had to be calmed before she caused the destruction of the whole world. The Yoruba deity Oshun was shunned but created abundant life anyway. She is sultry, vibrant, warm, creative and a powerful orisha. But she is not immune to vanity.

Some of the goddesses and spirits in this book are truly dark. Like Baba Yaga, some of them eat children. Like the krause, some of them are grotesque, just for the sake of terrifying others. They do not need or want acceptance. They exist and that is enough for them to thrive.

Invoking goddess energy isn't only for those labelled as female. We all have masculine and feminine energy within us. These tales of the dark feminine are for all times and for all genders. The ability to create from shadow, transmute pain and rise to be the most powerful version of oneself is something we all need. Like water, energy can exist in many forms. And the heart, mind and spirit we each possess can be fertile ground for creating our own powerful dark energy.

As a writer of horror, I am firmly invested in the old tales, the first feminine origin stories. Those archetypes and tropes we still use today first began with a story passed on to someone else. As a woman from Mexican heritage, storytelling is something that has been part of my life since birth. I heard about fearsome creatures and urban legends, but they were all part of the oral tradition and nothing was written down.

One such tale that I loved was about the Donkey Lady who haunts a bridge in Texas. It is said you can see a woman who looks and sounds like a donkey, with feet and hands like hooves. The story was told over a meal or at bedtime, and like the tale of the child-murdering La Llorona, it was sometimes used to frighten me when I was misbehaving. "Stop it or the Donkey Lady will come get you!" Fast forward to adulthood, and I have created my own library of books about fierce women, both human and monstrous, because I love exploring the dark feminine. There is a gold mine of storytelling in mythology waiting to be rediscovered. In my novella *Goddess of Filth*, I use the trope of possession to express aspects of the Aztec sin-eater Tlazolteotl. Could demonic possession sometimes have a positive impact by creating change?

In *The Queen of the Cicadas*, a hate crime is heard by Mictēcacihuātl, the Aztec queen of the dead (whose tale also appears in this book). She is magical and terrifying with her flayed visage. I wanted to subvert the constant representation of the Virgin Mary as the pinnacle of womanhood and what is considered "good". Many of the old spirits and goddesses are multifaceted creations that stretch the boundaries of spirituality as dictated by the Abrahamic religions.

Another book of mine, *The Haunting of Alejandra*, explores post-natal depression through the myth of La Llorona, a woman who killed her two children and herself. She wanders in the night, crying and looking for wailing children to consume.

The horrifying tales that were once told to explain a terrible drought or devastating storm can still be used by us today to express tough experiences and emotions. We can describe and perhaps better understand our internal famines, winters, griefs and personal transformations through storytelling. Through goddess energy we can stomp on patriarchy and reclaim ourselves body, mind and soul. And subverting patriarchy doesn't just fall on the shoulders of females. It benefits everyone if we live in a more equitable world.

In times of uncertainty we can dig deep into the dark feminine and, like the Hindu goddess Durga, arm ourselves with many weapons to provide protection for ourselves and others. The Jewish and Mesopotamian demonic figure Lilith is about choice. Her energy is free will, and that is innate in us, too. We can choose to go a different path and not accept the labels, false narratives or shame placed on us for being who we are.

The dark feminine deities and spirits in this book are only a handful of many. Some you may have heard of, and others could be new to you. I hope each one will give you insight into the cultures in which they originated and insight into what they represent beyond being just an interesting legend passed down through the centuries. Most of the stories have multiple variations from different times, locations and cultures. I have chosen the tales I felt resonated most with our modern era, and in retelling them I have blended elements of the different versions because at the heart of each goddess identity is her story. That is the ultimate lure. We all love a good story. And we all have our own story.

Some of these deities are still worshipped around the world today. They and their devotees deserve respect, and I have tried to handle their tales with care. Enjoy these stories of the dark feminine and please share them, as they were created and passed on for that very reason.

KALI

Raze It to the Ground

The battlefield had been laid waste by the vicious fighting between Durga and the demon Raktabīja. Even the sun took fright and hid behind the dark clouds that rumbled overhead. The gods had called upon Durga to slay this arrogant demon who had brought chaos to the universe. They had entrusted this mission to her, and she would accomplish it.

Slice after slice, with her multiple weapons in many hands, Durga wounded the terrifying demon and strove to land the final blow. She would not stop until he was slain, but still Raktabīja lay on his back laughing with a hideous shriek that made the very earth move. His mouth of jagged daggers for teeth glistened with blood. His cruel eyes showed no fear of Durga. She took a step back, not knowing why he found this battle so amusing. His belly trembled, streaks of blood oozing from his cut flesh. The crimson droplets rolled slowly onto the earth like parasites looking for a host. Crying with laughter, the demon made his own wounds gape open and bleed even more. It was as if that had been his plan all along.

And then Durga understood. She should have known this vile creature would find a way to cause more mischief and make himself undefeatable. From every drop of blood that wet the earth, a small figure was forming. First a head, then an arm, then a leg ... until it became clear there was more than one Raktabīja. He was building an army of Raktabījas. Attempting to kill the demon would only ensure his survival.

He looked at Durga, his face smug. "You see, there is no defeating me. Even a goddess like you is not superior to me! You will all be mine to command."

He looked toward the sky where he knew the gods listened and watched with baited breath. "Do you hear me? All of you!" he cried, his voice pure vitriol.

More and more demons sprung from the ground, ready to fight for their progenitor. They gnashed their fangs and fought among themselves, their very nature to be agents of chaos. Fighting was in their blood.

The universe depended on Durga's victory, but she knew she could not do this alone. A truly formidable challenger was needed for this impossible task. She fixed her gaze upon the hideous demon and narrowed her eyes, focusing all her intention on stopping him. The flesh between her eyes began to ripple and morph, like the belly of a woman heavy with child. First a hand could be seen, and then the outline of a head. Durga squeezed her eyes shut, the folds of her forehead becoming more pronounced. A slit of flesh became a deep, dark well. From the darkness within Durga's body, Kali pushed through flesh and skin and tumbled to the ground. Her loose, wild, black hair covered her naked body until the newborn goddess rose to her feet. Jet black skin glistened with the dew of birth. She carried a noose and a sword in her hands.

Kali's eyes glowed with incandescent red fury and darted from one demon to another. The demons stared at her, poised to attack.

The goddess opened her mouth and let her thick, red tongue emerge from between her lips. Snarls and growls rose from the demons as they felt her threat.

Raktabīja glared at Kali. "I am not afraid of any god and I am certainly not afraid of you!" he hissed. He wiped his mouth and flung the blood onto the ground. More demons wiggled out of the earth like starved maggots on a carcass.

Hungry for destruction, Kali set upon the small demons sprouting from the soil. One by one she began to devour them with an insatiable rage. Her sword severed limbs and heads. Bones crunched between her teeth as she consumed flesh and blood with the urgency of the starved. The more she ate, the faster she whirled, steam rising from her skin. The gluttony of blood and flesh fed her lust to destroy all before her. Her appetite was all she knew now. Her eyes had become mirrors of chaos. The path had to be cleared, and Kali was the agent of destruction. It was what she had been birthed to do.

The remaining demons ran toward Raktabīja, fear now in his eyes. As she neared him, Kali licked her lips with her long, red tongue and swung her blood-smeared sword. She picked up her pace, snatching up the demons like insects. Some she chewed and others she swallowed whole. None could get close enough to inflict harm upon her without becoming a meal themselves. Their numbers thinned and the din of their hisses and shrieks quietened, until only Raktabīja was left. Thunder clapped within ink-black clouds, as dark as her skin. The storm raged along with Kali.

"You can't just eat me! You are not that powerful!" the demon screamed in disbelief, but this only enraged Kali more. She raised the noose and swung it in the air, gathering the wind like a whirlpool above their heads. As he tried to crawl away, she sent the noose looping toward him and caught his foot. With one hard yank toward her, Raktabīja lay at her feet.

Kali's tongue lapped up the demon blood dribbling from her chin. "I will kill you!" Raktabīja shouted. He bared his claws and attempted to disembowel her, but he could not match her speed. She grabbed his head, her fingers digging into his flesh. His eyes bulged as she squeezed harder. In a single bite, she removed his head and drank the fountain of blood spewing from his neck. The demon's body became a loose sack of skin as she devoured him before any other demons could be created. After every drop of blood had been drunk, she ate up what remained of him. Her belly growled as Raktabīja was digested inside her.

The demon gone, Kali's blood still boiled with lust. She thrashed around in search of more destruction, her sword and noose flying through the air in her frenzy. The earth shook with each step she took. Her rage had gathered an unstoppable momentum, threatening the peace that had been created by the death of Raktabīja. Her fury was great enough to destroy the universe.

"What do we do?" Durga cried out, her words lost amid the thunderclaps and Kali's earth-shattering stomps. None of the gods answered except one. Shiva appeared beside Durga and gave her a knowing look. Without a word, he ran toward Kali and lay down in her path. He closed his eyes and lay placidly on his back, his serpent coiled peacefully around his arm. Kali lifted one foot high in the air to crush the god, but when she looked upon his face, she recognized her husband. Her fury left her body as her foot touched his bare skin. The storm overhead subsided, the tornado calming to a breeze. Rays of sunlight broke through the clouds. Kali's body ceased its trembling, and her arms fell to her sides. For the time being, all was safe and as it should be. The demon was defeated, Shiva had bestowed his sense of peace upon Kali, and balance was restored.

Durga looked around at the wasteland created by the battle. This place had been razed to the ground, but it now offered the promise of new creation.

Kali – Born for Destruction

Kali is often depicted in Hindu art as she appears at the end of this story. She stands over Shiva with one foot on his chest following her victory over Raktabīja and the subsiding of her bloodlust. Shiva is Kali's counterpart and is associated with the colour white, while she is either ink black or blue. She has three eyes, and at times she either has ten arms or only four. She always wears a garland of decapitated heads around her neck, and a skirt of severed arms. An exposed thick, red tongue and fierce eyes to match add to her ferocious look, as does her wild hair, always loose and flowing behind her. She carries a severed head and a plate to collect the dripping blood. She is also known to carry a sword and a trident. However, centuries before becoming a goddess in her own right, fearsome Kali was merely one of the seven black tongues of a greater fire god called Agni.

The legend of Kali and Raktabīja is a powerful one, because Kali is the goddess of death and destruction. In Sanskrit, the root of her name means "time" or "black". Time is certainly our destroyer as we die with age, but Kali can also bring death to the ego in order for us to transcend the trappings of this world. It is no wonder she is worshipped in cremation grounds, as is Shiva. However, Kali does not only represent death. She is also seen as a strong mother figure and is worshipped as a protector.

In *Indiana Jones and the Temple of Doom*, the gruesome Thuggee cult participates in human sacrifice in Kali's name. She is not actually portrayed in the film, but we are given the impression she is not "good", as "good" would be defined in the simple terms of a figure such as the Virgin Mary (there is no question about Mary's "goodness", no duality in her character). An ancient goddess with the power to destroy the universe is anything but simple; if Kali is not "good", then she is not "evil" either. She can't be blamed for her adoption by the Thuggee cult, and in any case, historians now question whether those murderous Kali-worshipping bandits ever really existed or whether they were just a colonial fabrication.

Kali is an emanation of Shakti, embodying creation through destruction, and Durga (who we learn more about later in this book) is also associated with it). One who possesses Shakti cannot be limited to a unitary description or a single purpose. Shakti is feminine energy at work, the mother goddess from which all flows. Shakti is creation, destruction and movement springing from the divine feminine. Kali, embodying Shakti, transcends time and death, but she is also part of them.

Kali's ancient origins are described in the Rigveda. To immerse yourself further in her lore, you can explore the Devi Mahatmya in the Markandeya Purana. Kali is still celebrated across the globe today, offering her devotees empowerment and solace.

Kali Wisdom

Do not fear endings. Do not fear the smell of ash nor the smoke rising from the ruins. Nothing lasts forever. See each ending as an opportunity for something new, and possibly something even better than you can imagine right now.

We can use the ancient concept of Shakti to give ourselves the full agency of our minds and bodies to fulfill our dreams. Shakti gives us the courage to walk our path authentically and feel fearless no matter what challenges may arise. Like Kali, we can use our rage as a creative force to remove obstacles, start a new path or nurture something deep within that feels like it must burst out of us.

LILITH

The Road Out of Eden

Lilith had to leave. Yes, they had both risen from the same dirt and gasped for air in simultaneous coughing fits. When their vision focused, their eyes met. It felt comforting not to be alone in those first moments. In a flash she found herself aware and the awakening had her wondering what she was experiencing. She looked at her hands and touched her face, her body. Then she looked at the other, who stood in front of her.

The other appeared like her in some respects, but was also different. They both had long hair, and hair grew on their bodies; however, below and above the waist did not match. For a moment they stared at each other, studying each other's presence. His lips trembled and mouth moved until sound came from him. It was a grunt, which he followed by cocking his head to one side toward a pleasant trickling noise. He rose to his feet and walked in the direction of the noise, and she followed. She wanted to know what this place was. And were there others, like them?

They wandered the lush gardens, the grass soft underfoot, until they reached a river. She looked at her reflection. The soft curves of her body made her smile and her cheeks felt warm. She wished another had been made exactly like her. She touched her body, feeling the smoothness of her skin around her belly, then the soft hair between her legs. Inside it tingled when she explored with her fingers. She allowed her hands to roam her own form until the other moved close to her.

He placed a hand on her breast. She could see his body below the waist change, but she felt nothing when looking at him or at what was between his legs. He stepped even closer, wanting to touch more of her. But she didn't want him to. She was not the least bit interested in his body. This was not how she felt peering at her own image in the water. She wanted to be closer to a body made like hers. She felt a longing deep inside that she had no words for. It burned between her legs and deep between her breasts.

She pushed the other's hand away and began to distance herself from him. His face appeared puzzled, and he came after her. She followed the path of the river through the garden, not knowing where it would lead or how long she had to keep moving, but not wanting to stay there with him. Just as the river knew in which direction to flow, the instinct to leave that place guided her steps. The river changed from a calm and placid ribbon to a torrent of jumping white foam, crashing against rocks. There were fewer trees and plants here, and the ground underfoot was drier and rocky. The stones hurt the soles of her feet. But she continued to walk and he followed, his face becoming harder. The river slowed again and spread wide until the horizon was nothing but water. They had reached the edge of the garden. On her left was the ocean; on her right, a barren desert.

He extended his hand to her. She still did not want it. She wondered what was beyond the dry earth and limitless water that melted into the sky at the horizon.

She looked at her feet. A jagged crack stretched across the land, dividing one world from the other. This was where she had to make a decision. The other looked at the crack, then back to her. He drew back his hand. He would no longer follow her. She stepped over the crack, one foot still in the garden where her existence had begun. Instead of trying to keep her there, the other turned his back and walked in the direction from which they'd come.

An overwhelming sensation of relief washed over her. She looked into the dry and barren land. She felt afraid, but not as afraid as she did of having to remain in the garden, never knowing what existed beyond the touch of the other, that strange creature who was like her but also different. She moved her foot across the crack, then began the long walk into the unknown.

Lilith – Beyond Faith

Like Hecate (who appears later in this book), Lilith is a contemporary feminist icon, celebrated on social media and popular among those interested in witchcraft. It is the energy she represents that captures and keeps our interest. She is the rebellious first wife, the succubus, the rule-breaker and an all-around rabble rouser. A good source for reading more about her modern influence is *The Coming of Lilith* (2005) by Jewish writer Judith Plaskow.

In some Jewish legends, Lilith was the first wife of Adam, but she lacked the obedience to remain by his side in the Garden of Eden. Other Jewish traditions, however, do not include her. In ancient Mesopotamian mythology, she is more akin to the demonic goddess Lamashtu. Lilith's name is found in various texts – the Dead Sea Scrolls, the Hebrew Bible, the Babylonian Talmud – but these mentions are frustratingly generic and subject to multiple interpretations. Unlike those goddesses with a very strong identity, Lilith remains shrouded in speculation and debate. That does not detract from what she stands for.

In the anonymous medieval Hebrew text known as the Alphabet of Ben Sira, Lilith is Adam's first wife but she leaves him because he requires her to always remain beneath him during sex. She resists his dominance, believing they are equal, as they were both created from the earth. When he becomes insistent, she leaves for the Red Sea. Three angels are sent to her because God has decreed a hundred children will die every day if she does not return to

Adam. Lilith tells the angels she was created to harm babies and asks them to leave her alone. (According to legend, she can harm male babies for eight days and female babies for twenty, but if the children are wearing amulets bearing the name or image of the angels, she will not harm them.) She agrees that a hundred of her children – demons – will die every day. This tale reinforces the idea that Lilith's energy is hers alone to wield, and also shows how Abrahamic religions portray women who do not submit to the traditional role of a mother as being monsters or Jezebels.

Lilith Wisdom

Always walk away from people, places and things that benefit from your silence. Playing small to be more convenient or relatable is not the way of Lilith. Like her, you do not exist solely to help others at your own expense. Lilith energy isn't about being "chosen". It's the opposite of the "pick me" who thrives on the temporary thrill of external validation. Lilith isn't afraid to create a path where there isn't one. The unknown is merely a blank slate where you can create a new vision using blind faith. Faith in yourself.

Lamashtu

The Petitioners of Death

Her throne was made from the bones and skulls of children who didn't survive war, disease or famine. Small black sockets peered out into the void. Some of their mouths didn't have teeth yet. The row of mouths on the top of her throne held thick, white candles that were never extinguished. These were the everlasting flames of death and destruction that had tormented humanity since they set foot on land.

Some of the mothers prayed to Lamashtu to take their children rather than have them suffer the cruelty of what it meant to be human. No one wanted to call nature unkind, so she filled this role without feeling it a burden. She took their children without care or remorse when they wailed for it to be done. And now there was a place where those tiny bones could be laid to rest for eternity in peace, with others just like them.

When the uncontrollable forces of life overwhelmed these fragile humans, they attempted to regain control by calling on her or others like her, depending on their needs. Women cried out for her to take their unwanted unborn babies. She gladly ate them when the women slept. She left just enough so that when the petitioner least expected it, blood would leave her womb as a sign it had been done. The unwanted flesh gave her nourishment and the mothers peace of mind. What a burden to be born to a mother who didn't want you.

Sometimes women petitioned her to eat men who forced a child inside them. They wanted these evil males to experience the same terror they had brought into women's lives. And she did this with joy. She ate their meat and bones and drank every last drop of their blood. No evil deed goes unseen, so beware of those who do not fear invoking a demon for vengeance.

When she emerged from the shadows, the horror of her image was revealed. Her oversized head took the form of a hungry lion with bristling whiskers and yellow eyes, but instead of fangs her teeth were large and square like a donkey's. They could smash through a skull in a single bite and make bone a milky paste in her mouth. Her ears were also those of a donkey and hung low toward her mouth. Her entire body was covered with coarse hair and her feet were taloned like a bird of prey's. They matched her elongated human fingers, capped with nails as sharp as blades. She used them to shred her victims to fine strips. Sometimes she killed without being asked. She wanted to do it. It pleased her and it was the way she had been born. Her nature.

The sun had set, and the time had arrived for her to awaken to listen to the petitions of believers. She walked to her fountain of blood carved from limestone beneath a canopy of date palms. Two double-headed snakes, her companions, curled around the branches of the trees. They accompanied her whenever she rode in the night. Like the candles on her throne, the fruit and blood were always present. The dates never rotted, nor did the crimson tap stop flowing. She touched the blood with the tip of her nail. The concentric ripples released whispers that called to her by her seven names. The first was a prayer to bring a landowner nightmares to take away his restful nights. This type of torture happened to be one of her specialties: the vicious cycle of exhaustion and night terrors made for an entertaining show. Night after night, she wore the human down until they were driven to the brink of delirium. The very thought filled her with excitement.

A snort behind her made her look toward her throne. In a corner of the floor lay the boar and hound she suckled three times a day. She had found them near death on one of her many lethal journeys and decided to spare them for her own companionship. Next to them was the donkey she rode upon. She preferred donkeys to horses because they didn't frighten as easily, recognizing Lamashtu's teeth as being like their own.

She would allow them to rest a few hours more before it was time to move in the darkness and let the nightmare of her existence be known in all its beautiful cruelty.

Lamashtu – Angel of Desperate Prayers

Ironically, the Mesopotamian deity who used to protect against the demon or goddess Lamashtu is Pazuzu. He was made famous in the book and film *The Exorcist*, in which he possesses a child and proceeds to behave in ways characteristic of Satan in the Christian tradition. In reality, Pazuzu amulets were abundant and used as protection by the Assyrians and Babylonians for various reasons, including against the malevolent intention of Lamashtu. Amulets with her own image were also placed in homes as protection against her.

Lamashtu's father is the great sky god Anu, but beyond that she is her own woman, or rather, her own goddess. She has no consort, nor any offspring.

She features in the most recent Exorcist film, *The Exorcist: Believer*. Humans have always loved a truly scary story, especially one that strikes the most vulnerable, and Lamashtu is testament to that.

Lamashtu Wisdom

Not everyone will like you. You might be the villain in someone's story. Then others might see you as a friend, or as the answer to their prayers with whatever gifts you may have been blessed with. Whether they seek advice, a favour or something bigger, only you could be what they need in that moment – and that is a privilege. When someone is described as being in their "villain era", it usually means they don't hide their so-called nasty side behind beauty or feigned sweetness. They just let whatever is perceived of them be, even if it comes across as evil or unkind. There is a swagger to owning perceived badness. And it's better to be a villain than to be two-faced.

Beira

Crone of Winter

Beira's countenance was as hard as the stones on the mountain peaks where nothing grew. Her heart was as frozen as the lakes in midwinter. Her desire to remain in perpetual winter showed in her icy gaze. In the frigid night, she stalked the village until she found a beautiful maiden in the spring of her life. Through the window, she watched the maiden sitting by the fire with rosy cheeks and bright eyes. Beira tapped her staff on the ground, causing a cold wind to move like a clawed hand beneath the door. Ice covered the window and the floorboards until it reached the hearth inside the cottage, and the finger-like eddies of the frigid wind snuffed out the fire in an instant. The door slammed open, letting in a flurry of snow.

In the darkness she presented herself. Her blue lips curled into a wicked smile and her one eye blinked as she stared at the maiden trying in desperation to relight the fire. "There is no need for that, my dear," she said in her raspy voice.

The young maiden turned around and her eyes went wide seeing the giant hag hovering above her. The room seemed to shrink around her domineering presence.

"What do you want?" the maiden asked, her voice trembling. She shook from fear and from the icy cold. Snowflakes fell on her head and dusted the inside of the cottage.

"I want you!" Beira gripped the arm of the maiden. "What is your name?" the crone demanded as she brought her face closer to the girl's, flashing teeth the colour of filthy water and swollen, receding gums. Hairs sprouted from her nose and ears.

"My name is Bride."

Beira's face twisted in contempt. "Bride, you are now my servant. If you try to escape, I will freeze you to death. The snow will cover your body until it can rot in the spring. No one will mourn you."

Tears fell down the maiden's cheeks. Beira dug her nails into Bride's flesh and dragged her out of the house without any warm clothes to protect her from the cold. The maiden couldn't fight the strength of this goddess and the pain of her grip tightened by the second. Beira pulled her through the snow and into the depths of Ben Nevis, to work at her bidding.

It was dark and cold inside the mountain, with few torches to light the way. Icicles hung from the ceiling, slowly dripping into black pools and dampening the stuffy air. Beira brought Bride to a small room with a barred door. Inside, there was a hard bed covered in scratchy blankets. There was a hole in the corner of the room and a wash basin next to it.

"Get comfortable," said Beira. "You will be here a while." The crone shoved Bride into the cell and slammed the door shut. Iron keys clinked as they turned in the lock. Beira let out a horrid laugh as she walked away.

The following morning, the crone brought a bowl of gruel and glass of water. "Eat and then your first task."

She tossed at Bride's feet a filthy, dirt-caked fleece. The smell made Bride gag.

"Go wash this. Don't think you can stop until it is as white as the day I received it. And don't think you can escape. My powers cannot be matched by the likes of you," said Beira. Her mean eyes twinkled with hate.

Bride cried as she crouched over the stream in the forest, her hands bright red from the freezing water. She felt no hope of ever making the fleece clean enough to satisfy Beira. Her arms ached with every hard scrub. When her hands became numb, she did her best to blow some warmth onto them. It wasn't much of a comfort. And of course, the fleece didn't brighten much.

For three bleak, icy days she had to go to the stream and try to wash the fleece until the skin on her fingers cracked and bled. On the third day, an old man passed her. He had kind, blue eyes and a beard as white as the snow. He stopped, seeing Bride in tears. "What is wrong, dear?" he asked.

She dried her tears, embarrassed. "This fleece. It won't come clean and I must make it white."

He smiled and walked closer to her. "Let me see that."

She handed him the soggy, brown wool, dripping water onto his boots.

He shook it out three times, droplets of water flying through the air. The fleece turned brighter than any hue of white she had ever seen.

"How did you do that?" she asked excitedly. She wanted to cry with joy.

"I am Father Winter. It is what I do." He reached inside a leather satchel and handed her a bunch of perfect snowdrops. "Tell the one you work for that it won't be long now."

"Thank you! How can I repay you?"

"Just go."

She took the flowers and the fleece and rushed back to the mountain. In the great hall, Beira sat on her throne. "What do you want?" she screeched, meat and congealed fat dribbling from her chin.

Bride showed her the fleece and the snowdrops. Beira's eyes went wide seeing the flowers.

"Where did you get those?" she asked through gritted teeth, a glint of fear in her eyes. Bride threw the fleece onto the table. "Father Winter gave them to me. He said it wouldn't be long now."

Beira jumped to her feet and barged past Bride and out to her horse in the stables. She snatched up her hammer on the way. "There will be no spring!"

The old woman rode through the forest and fields thrashing down the new green shoots heralding spring. Winter would remain for as long as she wanted it to.

Far from the rugged mountains in the throes of winter was the Isle of Summer. Prince Angus Og awoke in a sweaty fit as the warm morning sunlight cascaded into his room. He'd had a dream he could not shake because it seemed, and felt, so real. He touched his chest, but the ache remained. Without bothering to dress, he made his way straight to his father to seek counsel.

His father was sunning himself on his throne near a window, the birds chirping outside. "Father, I've had a most vivid dream. There was a young woman. So cold and filled with sorrow, I could feel her heartbreak and longing. I must know if she is real or not."

His father looked at his son still dishevelled from sleep. "Yes, she is Bride," he said, his voice even and slow. "She cries because the Hag of Winter has kept her enslaved. But one day, she will be your bride."

Angus was shocked by this revelation. "What? Well ... why wait? Why keep her in pain? I don't know her, but I feel I already love her ... it's as if we are tied by some thread woven through time and spirit."

The king gave his son a stern look. "It is the month of Imbolc. You could die in the cold if you leave the Isle of Summer! Wait until the Queen of Winter has less power."

"No, father. I must do this now."

The king sat upright on his throne, his casual demeanor changed to commanding. His blue eyes were now like steel. "You will do as you are told and wait. Now, go make yourself presentable for breakfast."

Angus clenched his jaw and left his father. He rushed back to his room to dress and fill a small backpack with warm clothing. Without disturbing the servants, he stashed a loaf of bread, cheese and apples, and a water skin to fill at the well.

Before leaving, he snuck into his father's chamber and took the king's wand. He would return it as quickly as possible, and with luck his father would never know he had it. What was the point of magic if not to use it?

Angus fled on horseback. At the port, he took out the wand and borrowed three perfect days from August to calm the stormy weather long enough to reach Bride. As the sky cleared and seas calmed, he pushed forward as fast as he could to reach Ben Nevis.

It was a miserable journey, unaccustomed as he was to the snow and cold winds. Angus longed for the sun and his Bride next to him. Finally, he arrived at the mountain, where all seemed desolate and quiet, snow weighing heavily on the barren trees. He rushed through Beira's fortress crying out, "Bride! Make yourself known."

Hearing his voice, Bride jumped to her feet. "Here! I'm over here!"

He looked at her through the bars of the small window on the door. "The keys are on the left," she said.

He grabbed them and unlocked the door. "I know you!" she cried. "I dreamed of you last night." They jumped into each other's arms and held each other tight.

"My father wanted me to wait but I could not imagine you in this dark place for much longer. We must go now, before Beira returns."

When they made their way out of the mountain, Bride's footsteps melted the snow. She couldn't believe she was free from the horrid queen. Tears of relief streamed from her eyes and the teardrops that fell to the ground sprouted into violets.

"Spring at last," she laughed.

Bride and Angus decided to marry and never be apart again. They left for the Isle of Summer, but Beira was not done with them yet. When she returned to her empty fortress, she shrieked into the darkness, shattering the icicles inside. She stomped out of her gate to see if spring was truly arriving. It was. She despised the sounds of the birds heralding the coming warmth.

In her anger, she jumped back on her horse and whipped it until it had picked up enough speed to send dark clouds the couple's way. She banged on the earth with her staff to freeze it until the end of March. She blew bitter winds, but Bride and Angus remained happy on Isle of Summer.

The snow continued to melt and new life sprouted before Beira's eyes. Dejected, she gave up riding through the land and made her way by boat to the Isle of Summer. Her weary feet had just enough energy to find the Well of Youth. She peered at her reflection and touched her face. She could see that exhaustion had taken hold of her. With a trembling hand, she drank from the well and retreated to a wood. There she lay down and fell asleep until it was time for her to rise again.

  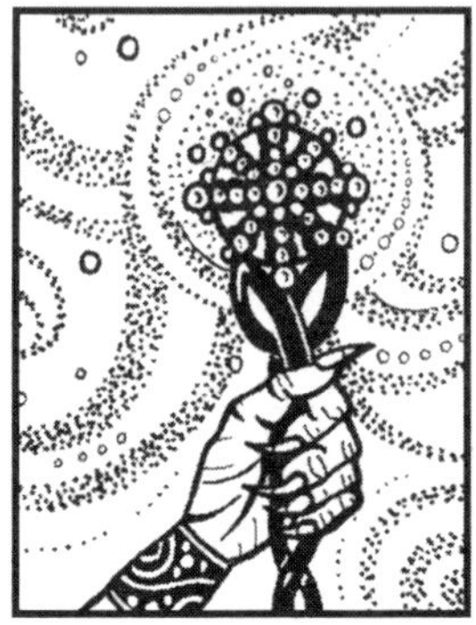

Beira – Coldest of Guides

Also known as the Cailleach, Beira is the Gaelic Queen of Winter, who dwells in Scotland during the frigid months. The landscape there is as treacherous as it is beautiful. She is associated with mountains such as Ben Nevis and Ben Cruachan, and with nearby bodies of water, such as Loch Awe (close to Ben Cruachan) which she created one day by accident when she forgot to cover her well and the water streamed down the hillside to fill the valley.

This book explores many goddesses who are known for their beauty, which is part of their power and lure. However Beira is not one of these goddesses. She is described as a hag, giant in stature with copper-coloured teeth, one eye, blue skin and snow-white hair. Her disposition isn't kind or benevolent either. She is as pleasant as a blizzard. But she is strong and powerful. She created the mountains and hills with her large hammer in one hand, and the staff in her other hand can freeze the ground where she taps it. It is also written that she is the mother of all the gods and goddesses. You can read more about her in *Wonder Tales from Scottish Myth and Legends*, published in 1917 by the folklorist and journalist Donald Alexander Mackenzie.

Bride or Brigid was a pagan goddess who became a Christian saint and is associated with Imbolc (1 February), the first day of Celtic spring. She travelled to the Caribbean to become Maman Brigitte, who features in the next tale.

Beira Wisdom

Our lives are guided by cycles. We cannot escape them. Know that even the harshest of seasons always comes to an end to make way for softer and warmer times.

But there is another lesson here. Do not fear ageing. It is a tale as old as time that the crone is hideous and ugly. Youth is sweet and perfect because the ravages of life have not yet had the chance to etch themselves on a body and face. Beira loathes the spring (youth) because she sees it as a threat to her existence. Like winter and spring, ageing and youth are equally valuable and part of being human. So love yourself, whatever season of life you are in.

Maman Brigitte

Tombstone Guardians

The sun had bled across the horizon and now surrendered to the darkness of night. Stone screeched on stone and the door of the grand mausoleum opened to the fresh night air and a sky full of bright stars.

"What a fucking time to exist!" shouted Maman Brigitte. Her fuchsia lipstick accentuated the fullness of her mouth. She didn't know what cemetery she was in, only that she had been called there by a devotee. All the places where the dead are laid to rest are under her protection. Her long, purple, crushed velvet dress hugged her curves as if the cloth had been cut with a razor to fit her body to perfection. Thick, fiery red curls brushed her bare shoulders when she moved. Her perfume of rose with a hint of clove scented the air. Sharp stilettos struck the stone walkway and the sound echoed through the quiet cemetery.

Not many people like a cemetery after dark, but it is the best time to visit, because then the voices of the dead can clearly be heard. Maman Brigitte met all sorts, and they told her their stories and experiences of life. Sometimes in death you can learn the meaning of really living.

She wore a gauzy black cape that grazed the ground, clasped at the neck with a ruby. Her breasts rose and fell as she inhaled a waft of cigar smoke. Baron Samedi, her lover and companion, was close. He too watched over the dead. On the ground next to the mausoleum a devotee had left an offering: a glass bottle filled with rum infused with red peppers. She loved this. The heat made her feel alive. She grabbed the bottle. There was also a plate of chocolate and plums, and a bottle of red wine. Black candles flickered in the darkness.

A woman's name was written on a hospital bracelet. Maman Brigitte kneeled down and touched it. This soul's prayers would be heard that night. But first she wandered through the cemetery to ensure all was well in her domain.

She glanced at the gravestones and read the names and dates of their lives. The time granted in this realm was as unique as a fingerprint and as mysterious as the universe itself. Small animals scuttled in the dark, but nothing else disturbed the peace of those laid to rest. In the distance she could hear music. It made her smile and want to dance. She swayed her round hips in the moonlight, relishing the sounds of the living making the most of their time to make love, cry, celebrate and engage all their senses. In the blink of an eye, they could be spending their nights with her. Their flesh would be gone and only the spirit of their memories would remain, along with those left behind to mourn, who would remember and perhaps call on the dead for ancestral knowledge and help.

Maman Brigitte opened the bottle of rum and sniffed the fragrant sweetness. The aroma of chili pricked her nose. The heat might make a mortal cry, but whoever left this offering put the right amount of Scotch bonnets inside. She took a long gulp and let it burn down her throat. She smiled and drank more. This bottle would be done by dawn.

"You make death a most beautiful destination."

She turned to the deep voice. There he stood, tall, with shoulders broad enough to carry ten headstones. His top hat shrouded his eyes, but she didn't need to see them. Wherever she was, they pierced her very soul. Just as the mere thought of her touch brought him running to her.

"My dearest Baron," she said in a teasing tone.

He walked closer, handsome in his perfectly fitted black suit with a purple handkerchief. An unlit cigar stuck out from a pocket, and he held a lit one nearing its end in his right hand. He smelled like smoke and burning autumn leaves. And her body burned for him, always. He tossed the cigar to the ground and pulled her close.

"Care for a dance?"

She threw her head back and laughed as the music in the distance turned to a sensuous tune. "I would love to dance."

They swayed to the music in the main walkway between the rows of graves, careful not to disturb the resting places. His hands moved to give her ass a gentle squeeze.

Her heart filled with joy as she lay her head on his chest that had no heartbeat. Her joy came from the scent of his presence and the knowledge that the two of them could comfort others once the dance of life was over. And also from knowing that she could aid those who called upon her when they needed a friend – someone to listen when things seemed as dark as night, who would encourage them to experience this life to the full.

The dance never ended, only the song changed after death.

Maman Brigitte – Protector of Cemeteries

She is a Loa – a god or spirit from Vodou, the African diaspora religion that developed in Haiti and other locations. Her feast day is celebrated on 2 February or 2 November. The latter also happens to be the Day of The Dead (Día de Los Muertos). Devotees can offer her pepper-spiced rum or black roosters which are also seen as protectors from dark energy in Haitian Vodou.

As shown in this story, Maman Brigitte is the guardian of cemeteries. Her consort is the top hat-wearing Loa of the dead, Baron Samedi. He too has a fondness for rum. They are both part of the Gede, a Loa family associated with death and fertility, cemeteries and music.

She can be petitioned for justice by those suffering domestic abuse or infidelity. Maman Brigitte also offers healing to those who are spiritually, emotionally or physically unwell, including the ability to cure sexually transmitted diseases. She is connected to the Irish saint and goddess Brigid (or Bride), who is also associated with healing – Maman Brigitte's February feast day is around the same time as Brigid's and they share the same name. Unlike the other Loa, Maman Brigitte is sometimes depicted as a white woman with red hair. Irish indentured servants and immigrants to the Caribbean were exposed to Vodou when working among Africans brought to the West by the slave trade, and Maman Brigitte is the result. This synchronization of beliefs resulting fron colonization is something that can be seen across various cultures.

Maman Brigitte Wisdom

Fuck it ... and celebrate! Now is the time to enjoy life because we do not know how soon it will end. The highs and lows are part of the experience. Embrace them all. Maman Brigitte reminds us that we are all heading for death from the moment we leave the womb. Like other goddesses, she teaches us that our lives are ruled by seasons. She wants us to enjoy all of it, no matter what part of the journey we are on. Squeeze every ounce of joy you can from this ephemeral experience.

Every day do one thing that brings you joy. You deserve that.

RHIANNON

Better a Goddess than Queen of a Mortal

The goddess had always been wild and her free spirit took her across the land on the back of her white horse. No man could catch her. She lived to ride, and horses were her first love. And so it was, until King Pwyll, unable to catch her on horseback, called out to her, asking her to please stop and talk to him. That was the beginning of her journey to becoming a queen.

Rhiannon had waited for a child for so very long. Ever since their marriage, her human husband King Pwyll had desired an heir. There were whispers about her being different and perhaps even cursed. Years passed and finally she gave birth to a son, Pryderi.

Both she and her husband were elated at the arrival. There would be no more rumours. They were now a family and, more importantly to Pwyll, an heir was secured.

"You will have all the help you need. Our prince will have only the best care."

"Thank you," said Rhiannon. She knew the staff well and trusted in their abilities.

A few weeks after the birth, she left the baby with the nursemaid as she did every evening before she went to bed. The woman, not much younger than Rhiannon, took the child into her arms. Sometimes Rhiannon would hear his little cries in the night as is usual for infants, but they would soon stop as the nurse took care of him.

"Sleep well, my lady," said the nursemaid.

Rhiannon kissed her sleeping son on the forehead. "Thank you. See you both in the morning."

She retired to her chamber for the night.

The sky was clear and a full moon illuminated the night. The nursemaid sat near the cradle, her eyes feeling heavier and heavier by the minute. The woman who usually helped her was ill, and so she'd had to bear the duties alone. The exhaustion had caught up with her. She tried to stay awake but her body fought her.

A loud thump roused the nursemaid. She couldn't have been asleep that long. She glanced into the cradle and panic gripped her body. She trembled at the sight of the space where the infant should have been. With rising fear, she jumped to her feet and ran to Rhiannon's room. She peeked in to see if the child was with his mother. Rhiannon was fast asleep and there was no sign of the baby. The nursemaid snuck into the king's bedchamber. He too was asleep, without the infant.

She ran through the castle trying to hear the faintest sound of a baby, but nothing. No one was awake.

She ran to the kitchen. The baker usually arrived early to begin his duties, but it was still dark and empty except for the family hound and her new pups. The nursemaid stared at the little things curled next to their mother. If she didn't do something drastic then she would be blamed and hung without mercy. She couldn't think who would dare take the child. All she could think of was her own skin and her own children left motherless.

She crept toward the hound and took one of the puppies. It didn't fight her, just squirmed a little. She grabbed a knife and a rag, then ran outside. In the moonlight, she slit the pup's throat and soaked the rag with its blood.

She left the dog in a bush by the castle to dispose of later. With the bloody rag, she ran back up to Rhiannon's chamber. As the goddess slept, the nursemaid wiped her hands and face with blood, and rushed away before she could wake. The moon was still high, and she had time to dispose of the evidence.

Part of her felt terrible for betraying her queen like that, but she was a lowly maid. She had children of her own who needed her. If she died, so would they. After she'd cleaned up, it was nearly dawn.

Rhiannon woke to screaming and loud voices. She opened her eyes to see her husband looking upon her in terror.

"How could you?" His eyes were red and full of fury.

She saw then her own hands and nightdress. She was covered in blood. The nursemaid stood next to her husband, sobbing.

The queen's entire body quaked at this senseless scene. "I don't understand ..."

"You did it! You killed Pryderi!" Pwyll shouted. The veins in his neck bulged and his face turned crimson. She shook her head. "What? No! No, no, no!"

Her mind and heart could not understand the false accusation. "Where is my son?" she screamed.

"You tell us where he is? What did you do?"

"I did nothing! Why would I do such a horrible thing?" she insisted.

The nursemaid wrung her hands. "There's no one else who could have done it. And look at you!' She turned to the king: 'I heard noises and went to check for robbers. When I got back, Pryderi was gone! I assumed the queen had him but I found her covered in blood. That's when I cried for help."

"You must be punished." Pwyll said to Rhiannon, devoid of mercy. "You will remain here until I say you can leave."

Rhiannon couldn't get her mind around the fact Pryderi was gone. And not just gone – dead. And they believed she did it! Rage grew alongside her grief.

"I did not do this. Someone is framing me. Go find evidence. You are the king! Find our son! Spare no expense."

Pwyll's face was sorrowful. "We have evidence already and it all points to you."

When they left her alone, locking the door, Rhiannon burst into tears. It felt as if her heart had been ripped from her chest. Her son had been taken and she faced a terrible punishment for a crime she had not committed. But no one wanted to listen to her. Not even the man she had placed her trust in. This betrayal added to her despair.

News spread across the villages that Rhiannon had killed and devoured her baby. Three days later, Pwyll came to see her. Rhiannon hadn't bathed or combed her hair. She sat by the window mumbling to the three birds that perched on the sill every day. She'd scarcely touched the food and drink that had been brought to her.

"You must repent. You must show everyone that you are not like us ... not human."

She didn't have the energy to look at him. There seemed to be no way to prove her innocence. "How?"

"By enduring something so cruel that it shows how much you suffer without the son you killed. You were a goddess and now you must show everyone how you have fallen."

She didn't know what else to do. Not one soul believed her. No one came to her aid or listened to her pleas. Every back had been turned to her. Unless by some celestial miracle her son reappeared, her fate was to be treated as though she was guilty and punished for the crime.

There was no other way to prove herself. "Tell me, then, what you propose."

He stepped closer to her. With his thumb and index finger he lifted her chin, so she had to look at him.

"First, you will make yourself presentable. You are a queen. Act like it. Then, you will stand by the gates and tell every visitor what you have done. Because you love horses so much, more than you love me or our son, you will become one. All noble visitors shall sit on your back as you crawl on your hands and knees to the castle."

"And if I do not?"

He smiled. In that moment he looked more appalling and ghoulish than anything the goddess had ever seen in this world or the Otherworld. "If you do not do this, then you will endure something far worse. My councillors are all very creative men."

She yanked her chin from his grasp. There had to be some hope in finding Pryderi. In her heart she knew he was not dead. She needed to survive in order to find out what had happened to him.

"Fine. I will do it."

Pwyll left without a kind word or look. She hated him and wished him dead.

Twenty miles from the castle, a nobleman who owned and bred mares had a big problem – one with the potential to ruin his fortune. Every time one of his horses gave birth, the foal would go missing in the night. After months of this, he decided to hide in the stables after the next birth to watch out for the culprit. He would make him pay.

The night wore on without incident until just before dawn, the darkest time. At first there was a rustling outside the stables. The mare that had just given birth snorted and shook her head. She seemed scared. The lord knew the thief was close. He was poised to jump on them when they entered. But it wasn't a person at all.

A monstrous claw broke through the stable doors. As the mare moved its body to protect the foal, the claw scrabbled deeper into the stable, searching for its prey. The lord shouted, his sword raised above his head, and ran toward the claw. His first cut didn't do much damage, but it frightened the creature. It retreated with loud shrieks, and the lord pursued it through the darkness until it escaped onto the hillside.

The nobleman stood in the black night, panting and filled with terror. From his orchard he could hear the faint cry of an infant. He followed the sound until he saw a baby swaddled in a fine gold blanket. He bundled up the baby and rushed back to his home. He and his wife had no children of their own.

"My dear wife! Wake up!" he shouted. The baby cried at the sound of his voice. Holding it tenderly with one hand, he managed to light an oil lamp with the other.

His wife rushed from their bedroom. She looked at the wailing infant in shock. "Where did you find him?"

The weary lord shook his head. "By some miracle. Whatever had been stealing our foals also took this child."

"Have you heard of any missing children?"

"Not recently." They both stared at the baby with soft smiles as the lord gently rocked him in his arms. His wife touched the child's chubby cheek.

"Then the gods brought him to us for a reason. We shall look after him. I will find a wet nurse as soon as the sun rises."

Years passed, as they do, and the child grew to love the horses in way that seemed otherworldly. His hair was gold and his eyes were a blueish green, quite unlike the hair and eyes of the lord and his wife. It was probably just a matter of time before someone questioned this. His riding technique and knowledge were almost unbelievable for a child of his age. The lord kept watch over the boy. Part of his story was missing and he couldn't stop thinking about it. Only in passing had he heard about the king's lost child, who was thought to have been devoured by his mother. She vehemently denied it. He wondered if ...

One day he decided to find out for certain, knowing that otherwise he would never be at peace. "We are heading to the castle," he told his wife.

"Why?" she asked. He hadn't shared his concerns with her because he knew how much she adored the boy. Now at last he revealed his suspicion that the abandoned baby had been stolen from the king and queen.

The small family travelled to the castle to find out if the boy was indeed the king's son. After so many years of suffering, Rhiannon's face was lined with grief and humiliation, yet her nobility could not be denied. Her blueish green eyes still sparkled and her hair, falling in a long braid to her waist, was the colour of honey. The lord looked at her and then at the boy. The resemblance was undeniable. His wife had tears in her eyes. She could see it too. Her lips trembled and she nodded her head.

The lord squeezed her hand and they approached the queen together. He took out the gold blanket. "Excuse me, but do you know what this is?"

Rhiannon looked at the boy and began to sob. She moved toward him with her hand outstretched as if she wanted to touch his face. He took a step toward her, then looked back at his parents, then at her again.

"Come with me," she said to the three of them.

They followed her into the castle, into the king's salon. The more steps she took, the more confident they were. She stopped in front of the king, who was speaking to one of his advisors. She didn't bother being polite.

"If this is not our son then he is still out there, but I believe this to be him."

She held up the blanket. The king gazed into the child's face. He could see his own features and the queen's, and that was the very blanket their baby had been swaddled in every night since his birth.

"How did you come by this?" he asked.

The lord bowed his head and recounted the story.

"Tell one of the guards to bring the laundress," Pwyll said to the advisor. "She was our nursemaid before."

Time seemed to slow down as they waited for her in silence. But it didn't take long before a guard rushed in with the nursemaid-turned-laundress. She gasped when she saw Pryderi.

"Is there anything you want to say to us?" the king demanded.

"It is true. I made it all up. That wasn't the child's blood. I fell asleep and he was gone. I was afraid of what would happen to me and my own children." She broke down in tears, begging for forgiveness.

The king glared at her. "I know what *I* would do with you, however I will leave it to the queen to decide."

Rhiannon looked at the woman with pity. Yes, she had endured a terrible accusation and punishment, but what was done was done.

"I forgive you, but you may not stay in my presence and you will never work for our family again. Go."

The nursemaid left the castle with her life but nothing else.

Pwyll turned to her. "How can you be so forgiving?"

She looked him in the eye. "As you said many years ago, I am not like you. And I also forgive you."

His face darkened as she said this and he averted his eyes. Then he turned to his son and a smile came over his proud face. He put his hands on the boy's shoulders. "Welcome home, my son."

He thanked the lord and his wife. "You shall be rewarded for this."

Rhiannon rushed to the boy and embraced him. She wept with the joy of getting her child back and the relief of knowing her name was cleared.

The boy's adoptive mother cried as she watched Rhiannon rejoice. The goddess touched her hand, "Thank you for caring for him. You may return twice a year to visit him."

"That is kind and generous."

Rhiannon hugged the boy again. "We have so much to learn about each other. I don't want to ever waste another day."

Rhiannon – Meant for More

Rhiannon is a Welsh goddess, associated with fertility, horses, the moon, and forgiveness. Her name translates simply as *great queen.*

She is often depicted with a white horse or on horseback. Three enchanted birds called the Adar Rhiannon are also associated with her. They are said to have the ability to make the living sleep and the dead rise.

Although she is a Welsh goddess, she shares the attributes of the goddess Macha from Ireland and the Gaulish goddess Epona.

She comes from the Otherworld, the Celtic universe of gods and spirits. You can read more about her in the Mabinogion, a collection of Welsh stories compiled in the medieval period.

Rhiannon Wisdom

It is one thing for someone to abandon you and another to abandon yourself. You are a goddamn goddess! A beautiful being with one life to do what you want with. They don't have to believe you and you don't have to endure their punishment. You can always say no. You can always choose to leave. If only Rhiannon had remembered her own goddess nature and realized this earlier. She might have found her son if she'd gone looking for him.

Rhiannon also shows us that forgiveness is a personal choice. Forgiving someone could take years or it could takes a moment. Perhaps you don't ever want to forgive.

Pomba Gira

Not Your Usual Guardian Angel

Carina looked at the painting of a beautiful woman in a red dress with a slit up her thigh. The painting's subject stared out with a seductive smile, her lips slightly parted. You could see her passion for living in her confident posture: hand on hip, chin slightly raised and a leg parting the slit in her dress. Deep in her eyes burned the secret knowledge of her experiences. Her brown hair was pinned up with a large yellow rose and fell loose to her shoulders in soft waves. The sign behind her belonged to a club that had really existed in Rio before a fire in 1890 destroyed it. This woman, Isabel de Santiago – Carina's ancestor – was shot during a fight in that very club. She had died, and in the blink of an eye all her dreams and passion had died with her. Her dark skin was like silk against the red of her dress.

The painting had been in Carina's family for as long as she could remember. An art collector had offered her more than she needed for a deposit on a new house, but it didn't seem right to sell Isabel, even if the painter was famous. Isabel had had a great affair with him that led to their untimely deaths. Now she was just a distant memory, a ghost of the past.

This painting was all Carina had left of her family's belongings now that she had sold off everything left to her on her mother's death. With both parents gone, her grief and loneliness weighed heavily on her. And now she was having to pack up her home because the owner had decided to sell. All she wanted was a place of her own. She felt like she worked her ass off and had nothing to show for it. But then again, this world seemed like it was short on miracles.

Carina's finger hovered over the laptop. There would be another way. She deleted the collector's email. This family treasure had to be preserved for her children. She imagined displaying it in her home, maybe creating a family altar with the painting as the centrepiece. She left her computer and went back to packing.

It was still dark when she got up to make sandwiches for her children to take to school. The heating took some time to kick in and the old house was still cold. Carina stared at the painting on the floor, propped up against the sofa. She was exhausted by the strain of trying to remain hopeful as she searched for a new home.

Through the kitchen window the sky was a blanket of hazy whiteness, like the uncertainty of what was coming next in her life. The ground outside was covered in frost. It was all a far cry from Brazil. Carina opened the refrigerator and took out ham and apples. "What I wouldn't give to be on a beach right about now. I just need a little luck."

"Stop feeling sorry for yourself."

Carina slammed the fridge door in fright. The voice didn't belong to any of her children, but it sounded familiar. She stared around the room.

"Did I stutter? You heard me."

Carina remained still, not sure what to do. Was this her stress talking? There was clearly no one there.

"You can talk to me, you know. I don't usually make myself known like this."

Carina slowly looked towards the painting, dumbfounded.

The voice seemed to be coming from the image of Isabel! The hairs lifted on the back of Carina's neck. She could feel the goosebumps on her legs.

"I ..."

"Well speak up. Don't be silent, woman."

"What the ... Am I losing my mind now?"

"No. You are losing your home."

A wave of unexpected emotion made Carina break down. She hung her head and let the tears flow. "Yes. I need guidance. I ..."

"Then ask ... I am here. Your pomba gira. Good thing you didn't sell me."

Carina knew those words. Pomba gira. And the voice sounded familiar because it had come to her the day her mother died, when the painting became hers, but she'd dismissed it as just a dream. All her life Catholicism had given her nothing in the way of comfort, and she didn't understand the other ways of having faith, of praying.

She stepped closer to the painting and kneeled down before it.

"Can you hear me?" Carina said aloud in disbelief.

"Yes. And you really can hear me. You felt me when you deleted that email. I tried to reach you in your dream too."

Carina shook her head. "But I didn't believe."

"Go back to Brazil. Enjoy your life. Then I want you to go to a place where I once danced. I know you like photography."

"I love it. It's my passion. But how could it ever be anything more than a hobby?"

"Take your camera. Show the world our culture. Let others live through your eyes and lens. We can work together, you and I."

"But the cost ... I need to move."

"Let me handle that. Look for the signs."

Carina touched the vibrant brushstrokes. She didn't care if she was talking to a painting while wearing a pink dressing gown at 6am. She wasn't alone. Isabel de Santiago had her back when no one else did.

"I will build you an altar. Thank you for helping me to believe in you."

"Do not worry. I didn't believe either until *my* pomba gira came into my life. We go on. We must."

Pomba Gira – Spiritual Bad Ass

Pomba giras are a group of Afro-Brazilian spirits who help devotees with love, prosperity, relationships and sex; however, this isn't all a pomba gira can assist with. She can be part of someone's spiritual team, supporting a woman's empowerment and emancipation. She is characterized by her feisty nature.

Just like us, a pomba gira has her own individual identity and personality. At times she has been depicted as a prostitute. In art, she is usually in a beautiful dress that shows her figure; or her statues may portray her as half-nude. She is revered in the Afro-Brazilian religions Quimbanda and Umbanda. Her male spirit counterparts are called exus.

Devotees petitioning their pomba gira will offer roses, food, wine, champagne or other heartfelt and beautiful gifts. There are various names a pomba gira can go by: María Padilha, Dama de Noite, Maria Quitéria, Maria Farrapo, Maria Malumbo, Sete Sais, Tata Malumbo, to name just a few.

Pomba Gira Wisdom

Your faith and spiritual practices are your choice. Maybe you have been handed a belief system because it is the acceptable way to conform or assimilate, or because that's just how it is. Children don't usually ask questions about these things. As adults, we have the ability to explore and choose. We can change or step away from something that doesn't serve us, especially if it makes us feel unlovable, unseen or just doesn't resonate. Today, many people combine practices from different religions. It is all down to you.

Pomba gira gives us the courage to ask for help. She makes us feel brave and supported, knowing there is a guiding hand on our shoulder.

KRASUE

Deep in the Heart of Thailand

Anna stood by the chicken coop and held her hand to her nose. Something had got into the enclosure and tore into three of her chickens. For some reason, the predator hadn't bothered with the rooster and the four chickens that had survived. But what kind of animal can open a gate with a metal latch? She turned from the gruesome scene of ripped feathers, bloody severed feet and what was left of the carcasses with all the internal organs gone.

It wasn't the only strange occurrence lately. She thought about the horses as she walked to the barn to get a shovel. Three days before, a heap of their shit had disappeared. Nothing was left. Something had taken it or eaten it – she couldn't be sure. She would go online and buy a cheap camera to record what happened after dark.

She'd felt so happy and fulfilled since she and Matt had bought the farm, although the work never stopped. They had recently relocated from London after Matt's firm had been contracted to build a factory. It wasn't easy for her to get a work visa, so they'd purchased the land to keep her busy. Perhaps she'd been a little too confident in thinking she had what it took to run a place like this.

She grabbed the shovel to bury what was left of her chickens.

That night, Anna tossed and turned, as the cat flap banged in the wind. Next to her Matt slept like the dead, if the dead could snore that is. The need to urinate was keeping her awake, and it wasn't just her bladder and the noise from the cat flap disrupting her sleep. Her mind kept racing to possible explanations for the dead chickens.

After using the bathroom, she went in search of a paper towel to wedge the cat flap shut. The hallway floor felt sticky and wet. Anna's steps were slow and steady. She wondered if Matt had spilled something – but he would have cleaned it up. The boards creaked beneath her feet. She didn't notice the red footprints she'd left on the floor behind her.

She could smell something foul and as she walked into the kitchen, the stench overwhelmed her. The window above the sink was wide open. As she moved to close it, she heard a clinking sound that could only come from the wine glasses on the shelves behind her. She spun around.

In the darkness of the doorway to the dining room, two eyes were glowing. Her heart quickened. The eyes moved a little closer and now she could see the face of a young Thai woman. She had film star looks with wide-set dark eyes and long lashes. Her skin had the flawless texture of a porcelain doll.

"Who are you? What do you want?"

The face moved out of the shadows and the grotesque sight made Anna scream. The lovely film-star head was hovering in mid-air, a trachea and a broken-off spine dangling below it. Two wet lungs expanded and contracted as the veins dripped blood down a trail of thick intestines. Shit and blood leaked into a pool that formed below the horrible thing. The beating of the exposed heart filled the room, while the glistening stomach sloshed with blood. Anna gagged and ran for the light switch. The head fled out of the open window.

"You alright?" Matt stood in the hallway looking puzzled as he stared at Anna. His eyes travelled to the floor.

Anna shook her head, terrified by what she'd seen but not believing her own eyes. "There was a woman ... a *thing* ... Maybe it's been eating our chickens."

He stared at the gore and covered his nose. "Oh, man. You think the one who got the chickens – she left *this*?"

Anna opened her mouth and then closed it again. Matt would think she was losing her mind. "Maybe. I don't know ..."

He rubbed his eyes. "I'll help clean this up."

Anna lay awake until morning, haunted by the image of the exposed organs. It made her feel sick to her stomach. Was it even possible for something like that to exist? Was she going mad? She wanted to ask Matt to stay home with her, but couldn't find the words to tell him what she'd seen.

She was woken by a knocking at the front door. It had to be Praya, the local woman who helped with the housework once a week. She got up and put on her robe to open the door.

"Hello! How are you?" Praya was in her sixties. She gave Anna a warm smile as she entered the house. "You look tired ..."

Anna tried to smile back. "Something strange happened last night and I didn't sleep well."

The old woman began sniffing and wandering around the kitchen. "What's that smell?"

"Oh, like I said, there have been ..." Anna stared at the place where the head had floated and the organs had dripped their vile contents.

Praya touched her arm. "You can tell me. Sit down and I will make coffee."

As the kettle boiled, Anna wondered if she should tell Praya everything. She was local and maybe she had some idea about what was going on.

"Well, I guess I should start with the three of our chickens that were killed and all the horse manure that was stolen. Then last night I saw a woman's head floating in here." Anna braced for Praya to laugh at her and call her crazy. But her expression remained serious.

"Just her head? Any other details? This kitchen smells of filth," said Praya.

Anna's cheeks turned warm with embarrassment. "A head with its organs exposed. The intestines touched the ground."

The old woman gripped Anna's hand. "A krasue."

"A what?"

"You are not from here. A krasue is a creature of the night, who feeds on animals and faeces. She appears as a floating head and organs."

Anna couldn't believe that what she'd seen wasn't just a hallucination or lucid dream. "It's real?"

"Yes. Very."

Anna took in this information. "So what do I do?"

Praya gave Anna's hand a squeeze. "You have to find the body while her head is out feeding. It will be somewhere close by. The krasue don't wander far from their bodies because it leaves them vulnerable."

"How will we find a body – it could take forever. Do I just have to put up with some gross ghost eating my chickens and coming into my house?"

The kettle whistled and Praya poured water into the coffee cups. "There is one other way. I can stay here tonight and we can wait. When she shows herself, we rip off her intestines."

The idea sounded repulsive to Anna. "But can she hurt us? Those chickens were torn to pieces."

"She won't hurt us. She is just a nuisance to humans. We will show her not to come around here."

"Okay. It's a plan."

When Matt returned from work that evening, he was surprised to find the housekeeper still there. Anna pulled him aside. "She's having some work done at her home. Do you mind if she stays here for the night?"

"Absolutely not." He gave Anna a kiss and gentle smile. "Any other weird stuff happen today?"

Anna shook her head. "No. I think maybe I scared it away."

He smiled again. "Tell me if I can do anything."

"I will." Anna knew she could never get Matt to accept the reality of the krause. And she wanted to confront the thing herself. This was her farm and her chickens.

The three ate beef noodles as Praya told them stories about the land and nearby villages. Matt went to bed early as it was the usual early rise for him. Anna and Praya stayed up in front of Netflix. As the clock passed midnight, it became increasingly hard to keep their eyes open.

They were woken by the sound of chickens squawking. The two women locked eyes then grabbed the axes they had stashed under the sofa. They rushed outside to the coop. Beneath the brightness of the full moon, the disembodied woman's head was gnawing into the stomach of a chicken. The slurps and gurgles, and the stench of the faeces leaking from the intestines into the dirt, made Anna want to vomit.

But this was their chance. They quietly opened the gate to the chicken enclosure. While the krasue was distracted by her feast, Anna lifted the axe and brought it down onto the place where the creature's intestines joined her rotten torso. The krasue shrieked, dark blood sputtering from her mouth. Her wild eyes glowed in the darkness. Her organs shook from her screams. Praya worked on severing the innards. When the viscera fell off, the two woman moved back as the krasue began to convulse and shower blood across the dirt.

"This is my farm!" shouted Anna. "Go and don't ever come back!"

The creature weaved through the air like a deflating ballon, emitting its foul smell. It let out one last shriek as it flew toward them. The women ducked and it passed overhead and into the night. Anna stared after it. "You think this will work?"

Praya shook her head. "It will only buy us time."

Anna turned to her, confused. "Time for what?"

Praya met her gaze. "Time to build a fence with sharpened bamboo and, more importantly, time to find the krasue's body. This isn't over."

Krasue – Grotesque Terrorizer

Though the names and origin stories of the krasue change depending on where you are in Southeast Asia, she is always a grotesque femme hell-bent on instilling terror. In the Phillipines, however, the manananggal is the only one of this kind that prefers humans to animals.

As in this story, the krasue is depicted as a head with a beautiful face suspended in mid-air with organs and viscera trailing from her neck. These sometimes include the heart and intestines and always the stomach. The concept is straight out of a nightmare or horror movie, and there are quite a few films with her as the star (the most recent are *Inhuman Kiss 1* and *2*, *Sang Krasue* and *Taman Krasue*).

She feeds on animals and excrement but not usually on humans, although in some versions of her story she devours placentas. In Thailand, one tale is of a Khmer princess who was meant to marry a general (some stories say nobleman) but was in love with a man of lower rank. When the affair was found out, she was sentenced to being burned alive. Before she could completely combust, she cast a spell over herself which could only save her unburned parts. Another legend tells of a sinful woman who lived a life filled with misdeeds and acts of evil, and who came back as a krasue after she died.

Krasue Wisdom

There are times in life when we walk around feeling like our guts are on show and bits of us have been torn away by painful relationships, regret and heartache. Life does take a toll on us after a while. Certain experiences have the ability to eat away at us. But can we reclaim our whole selves again? When we allow those old wounds to remain exposed, we don't just bleed all over ourselves, we bleed on those around us, too. It's unrealistic to think we will leave this life without wounds, but letting them fester will only leave us in pieces, searching for the missing parts of us in any scraps we can devour.

The only one who can make you whole is you. And when you feel complete, you don't need to search for wholeness in anything or anyone else.

EMPUSA

The Way Leads to Slaughter

The road crossed the hills near Athens and would end at the coast, where the two young men, Enops and Darus, were to find work on the merchant boats. Their parents had warned them of thieves and of the danger of accepting too little pay, but before he left, Enops' grandmother took him aside. Her dim eyes and rounded shoulders on a frail body belied the strength of her grip, which dug into the flesh of his arm. With fear on her face, she looked directly into his eyes.

"Be vigilant, especially at night, my dear grandson. There are things out there that can do more harm than any human."

Enops gave his grandmother a soft smile and patted her hand. "I appreciate your concern, but those are just stories. I've never heard of anyone actually meeting such creatures."

"She won't look like a creature at first! She will seem beautiful and enchanting, then she will suck the blood out of you. Your youth and strength are appealing to these ancient monsters. The Empusa awaits fresh meat like you."

He bent down and kissed her on the cheek. "There are two of us. I think we will be fine."

The men walked until sunset. They had encountered a few other travellers and a goat herder on the road, but nothing concerning. Everyone attended to their own business. They found a decent place to stop for the night: a grove of olive trees not far from the main road.

Darus started the fire and Enops brought out the dried fish and bread. The fire crackled and blazed merrily, keeping them warm as the night wore on.

After the small meal, Enops continued to drink from his wineskin. The wine made him feel drowsy. Darus had already laid down and allowed himself to snooze. A rustle in the trees caught Enops' attention. He grabbed his walking stick to shoo away any animal drawn to the fire or the lingering smell of food. The rustling turned to sniffling and whimpering. He lit one of their wax-topped torches in the fire and rose to his feet. The sound led him into the densest part of the olive grove, but he kept the campfire in sight, so he'd be able to find his way back.

Through the branches he saw a young woman with her hands covering her face. "Are you alright?" he called.

As he approached, she lowered her hands and looked toward him. Her eyes were the colour of the water surrounding the islands and her hair was like shimmering wheat. "I am lost. I should have stopped earlier, but I can't miss my boat tomorrow."

"Are you headed to the harbour?" he asked, moving yet closer to her.

She nodded and wiped tears from her rosy cheeks.

"So am I ... I mean, we. My companion Darus and I."

She continued to meet his gaze. He couldn't take his eyes off her mouth, her eyes, her body. Her dress touched the ground, concealing her skin, but his imagination was on fire. Her allure was magnetic, otherworldly, like lightening on a dark night. The sheer power of it made Enops feel closer to the gods.

"Would you care to join us? A young woman such as yourself shouldn't be travelling alone."

She gave him a demure smile. "Thank you. I'd like that."

Enops puffed out his chest, proud as a hero. "We are camped just over there. We have a wonderful fire and food and another wineskin."

He began to lead her back toward their sleeping spot, but after two steps he felt himself hurtling toward the ground. He bit his tongue as his chin hit a rock. It took him a moment to come to his senses. Had he tripped?

A hard kick to the ribs turned him over. The beautiful young woman gave him a sweet smile. She placed one foot on his chest. He screamed, seeing not a shapely limb but the hairy brown leg of a donkey. The hoof was caked with mud and manure.

"Whaaat ... what are you?" he shouted.

She moved the tip of her hoof beneath his chin and bent down to bring her face closer to his.

"I am your dream and your nightmare. And you are my sustenance."

Memories of his grandmother's warning flashed in his mind. "Please ... what do you want?"

She lifted her skirt higher to expose her other leg. In the light of the moon and stars, he could see the glint of metal. This leg was a dainty one, but made of copper.

"If you try to run, I will catch you and not only will I catch you, but I will make you watch as I devour your friend too. This is your choice and a very generous one."

He nodded his compliance. The Empusa took her hoof from beneath his chin and, straddling him, she sat on his waist. Despite his fear he could feel himself grow erect. She let out a loud laugh that turned to a guttural howl. Her body twisted and convulsed. Her sharp nails tore at her dress to expose her breasts. Her hips rolled and grinded on his hips as she ran her hands though her hair. The terror and eroticism of the moment made Enops cry. He couldn't take his eyes off her. She gnashed her teeth as she continued to rip off her dress. He felt himself close to orgasm even as her nails clawed and tore at her flesh to reveal a second skin, mottled with black spider veins. Her azure eyes had become black and red orbs, like a black night filled with blood. Her head lolled, then held still to stare at him. Hideous jagged teeth filled her mouth. The bones above her eyes protruded like a beast's. Her perfect taut breasts were now different sizes, the areolas grown as big as saucers.

"Do you still desire me? Because I still desire you!"

She laughed her vile laugh again, before opening her mouth wide and bashing her skull against his collar bone. A loud crack, followed by searing pain. His neck was in her jaws. Her teeth scraped at his flesh and muscle. Blood flowed into her mouth. A strange light-headed feeling was taking him over as he gazed at an olive tree. He just wanted to go to sleep and have this nightmare end. The gurgling sound of his own blood leaving his body lulled him to an eternal black rest on a lonely road where men and destinies died.

Darus awoke to soft whimpering. The fire had died down to a few embers. A young woman sat near him, hugging her legs. She was nude and covered in blood. He sat bolt upright. Her bright eyes tugged at his heart.

"Are you alright? What happened?"

Her body quaked. "I was attacked. I saw your fire and ran here."

He looked around. "My friend Enops, have you seen him?"

She began to cry. "He tried to help, but he was killed."

Darus reached for a blade. "Take me to him!"

She unfolded her legs and crawled toward him. Her hair hung down straight on either side of her head, grazing the dirt. Her breasts swung with a sensuous motion as she approached him. He put his blade down as he watched her move with the grace of animal.

"You don't need that. There's no threat now. Our assailant is dead. I shall take you to your friend, but first help me to get warm ... I'm shivering."

The low flames danced across her naked flesh and told a story of lust in the midnight hour.

"Of course, I will do whatever you wish. I have a spare tunic and when we reach a village, I will buy you clothing."

She gave him a smile as she nestled into him. "You are so kind."

"What is your name?" he asked.

Her lips brushed his neck. "I have no name. Only hunger."

Empusa – The Shapeshifter

Empusa is a shapeshifting entity, spirit or demon from Greek mythology. She is associated with Hecate, either as a spirit the goddess can command, or, some tales say, as Hecate's daughter. As her story evolved, she became associated with other types of succubus – the Lamia and Mormo. These are, however, distinct entities from different regions and the names are not interchangeable.

One of her legs was made from copper and the other was that of a donkey. She's most famous for being mentioned in the play *Frogs* by the fifth-century BCE Greek writer Aristophanes and in *The Life of Apollonius of Tyana* by the second or third-century CE Greek poet Philostratus.

In both accounts, Empusa is a frightening creature that travellers meet at night. Her stories also describe her as a beautiful woman who seduces men for their blood.

Empusa Wisdom

Your authentic self is the most beautiful version of you, reflecting your inner beauty and truth. Many times we wear different masks – disguises that we put on through life depending on who we are with and what we are doing. But there is only one true version of you, one inner authentic self. In all the shapeshifting that occurs in life, it is that manifestation of you that is the most valuable and powerful.

La Tulevieja

The Old Woman of the Forest

She was old, but she knew that. Most of her friends had already died and she never had any children. The older she got, the more invisible she became. When she went for a walk, she blended into her surroundings like the lizards in the forest or the insects on the rocks. Only when she seemed to be in a lot of distress or in need of help did someone notice. And even then, she had to ask. So the less time she had to spend at the village, the better.

The farm not far from her home provided goats' milk and cheese. She had her own chickens for eggs and their meat. Less than ten minutes' walk away was the river where she could fish if her back allowed her to do so, but fishing required standing or sitting for long periods, and this aggravated the muscles at the base of her spine.

There were no other chores that day except to collect kindling and logs for her little hearth. The best place to find fallen branches of the right size was by the river. Before heading out, she grabbed her large straw tule, a hat she'd woven herself. It protected her eyes from the sun and in the rain it kept her face and hair dry. It was perfect. Maybe the edges were a bit frayed and there were a few mud stains from when the wind blew it off her head, but she never left home without it.

It was late afternoon. She grabbed the ropes of her wooden cart and set off toward the river. The closer she got to the water, the clearer the voices of children became. She didn't mind children, but as she got older the younger ones seemed frightened of her. She couldn't help that her nose had a few too many blackheads, or that the grooves in her face had deepened with the years. Her eyelids were like curtains of flesh, hanging over her eyes. Her hair, once jet black, had faded to bone white. So she avoided children.

The old woman came to the river and began to scour the ground for kindling.

"Gross! Who are you? A *bruja* of the forest?"

She looked up. A boy about ten years old scrunched his nose at her. He was wet from playing in the river. He had a handful of rocks and mud.

She continued looking for wood so she could achieve what she came for and get out of there fast, or at least as fast as her body would allow.

A girl about the same age as the boy came running up. "Who are you talking to?"

"Her!" He pointed at the old woman.

"She's a *bruja*. Look at her ... that horrible old hat! La Tulevieja!" the girl screamed with laughter.

The old woman didn't have enough wood, but she knew it was time to go. As she turned away, something hard hit her. Clumps of mud slid off her arm. She looked up, stunned and hurt.

The girl began to chant, "La Tulevieja," over and over. The boy chimed in. Then two others came running. The four children circled her, chanting her nickname, making faces and laughing. She tried to break away, but they would not let her. One of the boys snatched her hat off her head.

"No!" she screamed.

They all mocked her. He ran to the river and tossed it in.

She shrieked at the sight of her beloved hat arcing toward the water and hobbled to retrieve it before it was lost forever. The ache in her crooked fingers would make weaving another one long and painful work.

The hat had caught on a rock. She could just about reach it from the bank. She inched closer to the water and stretched out her hand. Still not close enough! She began to wade into the water. The riverbed was slippery and the current fast.

"La Tulevieja!" screamed the girl. The woman jumped in fright and lost her balance. She tipped over and fell into the water. Laughter erupted, but it wasn't a funny matter. It felt like her ankle was broken. She tried to sit up but couldn't. The kids' laughter faded as they ran off.

A pool of red radiated from her leg. She glanced down. A bone was sticking out from her flesh. Pain began to crawl up her leg alongside the cold from the water.

"Help!" she shouted, as she looked around in panic. Not a soul was around. Someone had to come to help her. She could not hold herself above the water for much longer. The pain enveloped her entire body. She shivered and her eyelids felt heavy as more and more blood poured from her wound. In her weakness she could feel her body sinking into the water. It filled her nostrils and mouth, but at least the pain was subsiding. It was going away as she slowly fell into darkness.

The village was usually quiet after 9pm. Most people went home and the only place open was the cantina at the edge of the village, near the road leading to the city.

Manny got ready for bed. He was tired after a day at school and having fun by the river. He wondered what happened to that old lady. He was sure she'd got back up and gone home.

As he closed his eyes, his window creaked in the wind. His eyelashes flickered, but he couldn't be bothered to leave his cosy bed to shut it properly. Just as he was about to sink back into sleep, a large shadow crossed the wall. His eyes snapped open. It looked like ... a hat. The hat grew larger and larger, but no one was there. He sat bolt upright, ready to scream. He opened his mouth, but his voice was gone.

"You left me to die. You naughty boy. Now you will die too!" He tried to run from his bed, but his legs would not obey him. Then the old hag appeared: La Tulevieja. Slimy water dripped from her hat and hair. Her skin was a putrid green and pockmarked as if the fish and insects had made a meal of her. Her mouth opened to reveal a row of sharp, pointed teeth.

Manny was never seen again. The only evidence police could find at the scene of his disappearance was a small yellow strand of tule.

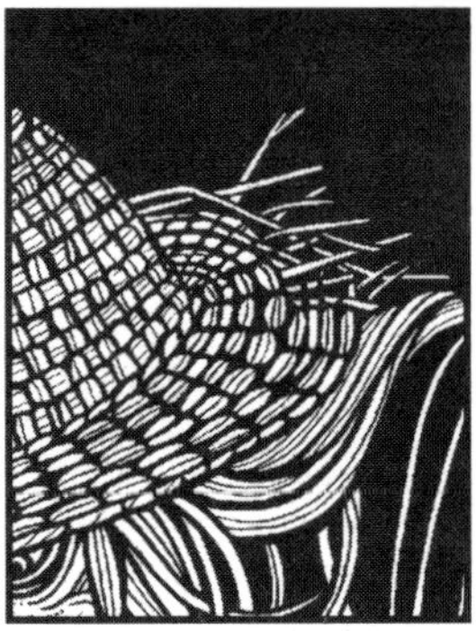

La Tulevieja – From Invisible to Immortal Spectre

Many variants of this story of a wronged and vengeful hat-wearing woman are told in Costa Rica and neighbouring Panama. In one version, La Tulevieja lures men looking for a piece of action. Her large breasts tempt them and that is when she strikes. In another, she is a promiscuous woman who likes to have fun, but becomes pregnant out of wedlock and kills her child. God condemns her to roam the earth forever for her sins, leaking milk from her breasts to feed her baby and weeping endlessly like La Llorona of Mexico (who murders her children and then kills herself). Obviously, this can be unpacked as a moral lesson teaching women not to have premarital sex, especially when practices such as abortion are not available or are considered sinful.

In Panama, the Indigenous tribe Ngäbe-Buglé have their own story that relates to the European conquest. An Indigenous woman called Tepesa has an affair with a Spaniard which results in an unwanted pregnancy. Her hat is all of her that is left behind when she abandons the infant to die.

I opted for this version of the story, which I felt I could relate to more as a perimenopausal woman. I value my solitude more than my youth. I don't feel the need to impress others and my priority is just to feel comfortable, considering all the changes in my body and mind.

La Tulevieja Wisdom

Ageing is the best reason to give zero fucks about what the world thinks of you. There is a sense that women become invisible after a certain age. They can no longer bear children, and if they already have them, then those children are living their own lives. Women in today's society are still centred as wives and mothers. They must first be desirable, then they must be fertile and then they must become mothers. After that, what use are they? Break away from that norm. You exist for you.

MEDUSA

The Making of a Monster

At the calm river's edge, with sunlight bathing her skin, Medusa sat combing her hair. She rubbed a drop of olive oil into the ends, then applied a palmful of beeswax from root to end, to give a brilliant shine. Her long honey-coloured locks fell to below her breasts like a silk scarf. She smiled at her reflection as she thought of love and of which handsome suitor she should choose – for she had the luxury of choice. This made her parents very proud.

"So, who will be calling for you today?" her eldest sister would tease, a hint of jealousy in her tone. But Medusa didn't care. Once she wed, her life's path would be set. She wanted to bear strong sons, yet longed in secret for a daughter. A daughter she could dress and whose hair she could comb by the water, like her mother did with her.

Today she bathed and prepared herself to give offerings at Minerva's temple. Her gossamer gown gave a hint of her fully blossomed figure. A body meant to bring life into this world.

The temple appeared quiet when she arrived. She liked this. There would be no one to disturb her as she prayed. The incense and smoke from lit torches gave the air a woody scent. She breathed it in and kneeled before Minerva.

"And what are you doing here?"

The voice startled her. She looked up and blushed to see a man taller than her father, with broad shoulders and a thick beard white as sea-foam. There was no denying he was attractive, but she had no desire to consort with someone she didn't know. "I have come for worship," she said politely before turning back to the statue of Minerva.

He stepped closer until he stood by her side and kneeled next to her. She glanced up and he gave her a sly side-smile. "Well, may I worship you? You are so very beautiful. I want to become lost in your hair."

His fingertip grazed the side of her face as he pushed away the hair that was covering her breast.

Medusa averted her gaze, feeling the intensity of his eyes. "I must go now." She moved to rise to her feet and leave, but Neptune grabbed her wrist. "So soon? Talk with me for a while."

The flush in her cheeks crawled down her neck and enveloped her entire body. This was not excitement. It was fear. She glanced around the deserted precinct, then smiled calmly and sweetly. She knew she needed to appease him until someone else arrived or she could get away.

"My parents will wonder where I am."

He pulled her closer, tightening his grip on her wrist until she was inches from his face. His breath smelled like dried fish and the sea. With his other hand he squeezed her waist. "Tell them you are with a god."

Her body trembled as she saw the coldness in his eyes, as dark and lethal as a brutal storm at sea. There was no warmth or care, only the crushing weight of his desire.

"Please let me go." She pleaded with her words and her eyes, hoping for some mercy. He could have anyone. Why her?

He smiled again. "No."

Without warning his entire body was overwhelming her, flooding her senses. She couldn't move, only scream. "Goddess! Anyone! Help!"

His tongue and limbs seemed to transform into tentacles she couldn't escape from. Searing pain made her scream until her throat burned. Hot tears rolled down her cheeks. She stared at the statue of Minerva, praying for release from the monster who ravaged her body on the holy steps of the goddess. He dug his nose into her hair, pulling at it with his hands, his teeth scraping her flesh. All Medusa could do was stay as still as stone. She wanted all life and warmth to cease to exist within her, and she wanted to be hard to his touch like stone, to feel unwelcoming. She wished her body to become cold marble.

And then he moved on top of her. She remained like stone. Her skin felt the cool air as her dress was ripped. What could she do now? What had been done was done. Nothing could turn back time.

Neptune looked toward the statue of Minerva and laughed before fleeing. He didn't give Medusa a second glance. She waited until she could no longer hear or smell him, then she crawled closer to the statue of Minerva with the little strength she had left in her body. At the feet of the goddess she looked up with tears in her eyes. Her broken voice croaked, "Where are you? Are you even real? Did you not hear me?"

As Medusa cried softly, hanging her head in despair, she felt a hand on her shoulder. "Your beauty is a curse. We are told it is a prize, but only so it can be won by the highest bidder or one who dares to steal it. Today it has caused you great pain. But I too am pained."

"I called out for you! For help!" There was a bitter note of betrayal in her voice.

Minerva's face darkened. "I am so very sorry, my child. You see, I cannot strike back at Neptune. He knows this so very well. No, it would start a war. But I can give you the power of the Gorgon while you yet remain human."

Medusa wiped her eyes. "I don't ..."

Minerva touched Medusa's hair still wet from Neptune's touch and the princess's own tears. "There will be a price. Many will say you are a monster and that I am a monster too, thinking I have punished you, but to be greater than a mortal woman is not a punishment. They will not ask who the real monster is here."

Her hand stroked the silken threads of Medusa's hair. "I shall transform you. If you wish."

Rage instead of tears burned red rims around Medusa's eyes. "Yes. What will anyone say of me like this? My family will be shamed. I am spoiled, ruined for anyone. I want my vengeance and I want to make him pay – to make all men pay."

"You may not understand it now, but you shall also have freedom. You will be feared by some and adored by others."

Medusa clasped her hands in prayer. "Yes, I want all this. Freedom from the shame that others cast upon me."

Minerva placed her hand on the crown of Medusa's head. "Venomous serpents shall replace your beautiful hair. You are more than a damaged maiden. You will become a maiden of death. You wished to become stone and now you wield the power to create stone from flesh."

Medusa's eyes rolled toward the back of her head. She tugged her long strands of hair and chunks of spun gold fell into her lap, a pile of human silk. She hunched over and felt her bald head. A puzzled expression crossed her face as an itching sensation crawled over her scalp. She cried out as from each follicle a writhing creature wiggled out and began to grow. The hissing became deafening in her ears, but Minerva held both of her hands, squeezing reassuringly as the tiny serpents swelled to full size. Their bodies lashed and whipped in every direction, their fangs on show. Strings of venom fell from their mouths.

"Do not fear, child. These snakes will not harm you. They are your companions and a sign of your power. Your kiss is venom and your gaze is lethal. No one shall ever hurt you again."

Medusa rose to her feet with Minerva's help. "Thank you, Goddess."

Minerva bowed her head. "Now go."

The Gorgon emerged from the temple, her body bruised, her dress torn and bloody.

She touched one of the serpents caressing her cheek, giving her comfort with its flickering, wet tongue. "Come my faithful companions. We have many miles to travel before we reach the sea. He shall weep an ocean for me – for all for whom the word 'NO' was not enough."

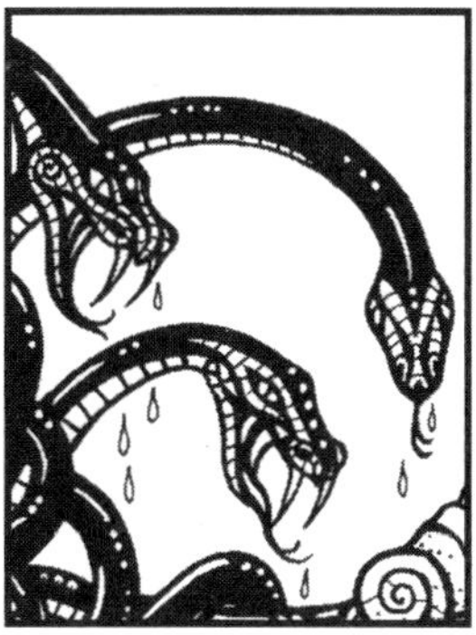

Medusa – Venom's Truth

This story is a retelling of *Metamorphoses* by the first-century CE Roman poet Ovid. The Greeks had their own version of Medusa. Instead of Minerva, the goddess was Athena, and instead of Neptune, Poseidon. Medusa gave birth to two children from her encounter with Poseidon: Pegasus and Chrysaor, who emerged from her neck after Perseus beheaded her. According to Greek mythology, the Gorgons were three sisters with snakes for hair and winged-serpent bodies. Different sources give different parentage to them. Out of the three, only Medusa was mortal, which is why she could be decapitated by Perseus. Her grotesque image is what turned men into stone.

Ovid's later version of Medusa's story tells of her being a priestess to Athena and so sworn to celibacy. Her rape inside the temple was sacrilege and angered Athena. In punishment, Medusa was transformed by the goddess into a hideous serpent creature so that no man would desire her ever again. Her head, severed by Perseus, was used by him as a weapon and was later placed upon Athena's aegis (shield) for added protection. So, she was punished for her rape and then her head was used to protect the goddess who made her a monster. It isn't my favourite version of Medusa lore, which is why I'm telling her story in my own way.

One of the best-known modern depictions of the hideous Gorgon of Greek mythology is in the classic film *Clash of the Titans* (1981). The film is showing its age in some of the Claymation-style special effects, but this just adds to the appeal for the cult following it still possesses. She is portrayed not as a woman with a head of snakes, but as a monster with scales for flesh, slithering like a serpent. Yet another version of Medusa, it gives an unforgettable face to female rage.

A Gorgon is neither mother, maiden nor crone. She is a power in her own right, making her own rules. Is this why Medusa must be killed? Because of the idea of such a creature possessing nothing men would want, yet being more powerful than them?

You can read more in the Greek poem "Theogony" by Hesiod and in Ovid's *Metamorphoses*. She is also featured in Homer's *Odyssey* and *Iliad*.

Medusa Wisdom

Medusa is autonomy and self-acceptance. When others curse us or speak ill of us for no reason except that we exist, or when they create a narrative that is not from our own lips, we must have the courage to be who we are and refuse to allow their venom to poison our self-belief. Do not change for someone who might shift their perception or opinion of you in the next five minutes.

When we turn inward, the world has less hold over our sense of our own value in society. Beauty is a perfect example of this. Everywhere we turn, we are told how to look, how much to weigh, how to dress or what gender should mean. But we get to determine these things for ourselves. Our personal power is strengthened when we can be who we truly are.

This is your experience. Live it for yourself.

Durga

Demon Slayer

The half-buffalo demon Mahishasura knew he had to pay his dues to Brahma. And he had done just that, for a period of time that would have tested even the most pious. Piety and calmness did not come easy to him. It wasn't his nature. The hair on his hulking chest and neck had become like a shaggy coat since he began his penance, fasting and standing on one hoofed foot in deep meditation for years. At least it looked like meditation, when in reality it was more like calculation.

As he stood in contemplation with his eyes closed, a warmth covered his body as if the sun had shifted to shine directly upon him. He opened his eyes. The god Brahma stood before him with all four of his heads turned in Mahishasura's direction. The white-bearded god had peaceful expressions on his faces. His voices spoke more-or-less in unison, with a slight echo. "I have seen your devotion since you began your penance. I would like to give you a boon. Make your request."

Mahishasura's dark purple lips curled to a smile. "That is so very generous. In fact, there *is* something I want very much ... immortality."

Brahma rubbed the loop of beads in one of his hands and sniffed the lotus flower he held in the other. "That is a rather large request. It is in the natural order of things that all creatures that live must die."

Being very clever and sly, Mahishasura had an idea to get around this. "Then shall we say neither a man nor a god can kill me? Does that suit you?" He asked this because to his knowledge, there was not one female human or goddess who had the power to stand up to him.

"Very well. As you have shown the good in you, your petition is granted." Brahma left as suddenly as he had arrived.

The buffalo demon put down his raised hoofed foot. Patience had given him exactly what he wanted. A loud burst of air released from his wet nostrils. Flat, wide teeth grinded as he thought of his plan. With near immortality given to him like a shield, he would be unstoppable. What fools the gods were! First, he had to gather other asuras, to create a fearsome and formidable demon army. He ran at immense speed from his meditation spot in the forest to begin his war. His thunderous footfalls made the birds and animals rush out of his way. Nothing could stop him or resist his desire for the throne held by Indra, king of the gods.

Mahishasura gathered his army in no time. Many asuras wanted to fight for their own glory, sharing their leader's egotistical nature and drive for discord. Human blood stained the earth as they ravaged the land. In the heat of conquest, his army's rage and ambition matched Mahishasura's own. The collective ferocity shook the heavens as cries of terror from the villages rose to the place where the gods resided. They knew there would be more trouble than they could contain.

Satisfied with the fright he had given the humans, Mahishasura made his way to Amaravati, the gods' capital city, where he would dethrone Indra and subjugate all the other gods who were helpless to harm him.

Intoxicated by power and bloodlust, the buffalo demon and his army crashed through the doors of the heavenly palace, Vaijayanta, and entered the sacred chamber to find Indra on his throne. The other gods were speechless at the bold move.

"I sit here now and none of you can stop me!" His laughter filled the chamber built from diamonds and gold. The gods cowered, knowing they couldn't kill him. Mahishasura's asuras snarled behind him, their weapons wet with blood. They were prepared to kill everyone in the room.

Indra and the other gods fled from the demonic horde to Vishnu's palace. Shiva and Vishnu looked at each other with deep concern for themselves and humanity. Brahma joined them in counsel.

"The only way to stop him is to kill him, but we male gods cannot do so.

Since his birth he has only been set upon domination and destruction. His penance was a mere ruse! We need a goddess to kill him," said Shiva.

Brahma nodded. "I agree. She must have all the best aspects of us to fight him, a warrior like no other. She will embody our power but wield it in a way we cannot. Her essence will be cutting power, piercing truth and blinding beauty."

Shiva, Vishnu and Brahma emanated all their power and ferocity into a new female deity who could slay the demon. She was the embodiment of Shakti. As this potent divine feminine energy took shape in a cloud of silky black hair, a beautifully radiant woman with ten arms appeared, dressed in red. The gods gave her many weapons to aid her mission, including a trident so sharp it could pierce through bone, a discus, a sword and more. All the gifts in her hands complemented the gift within – Shakti. She was their best and only hope.

Shiva approached Durga first. "We ask that you help us defeat the buffalo demon Mahishasura. You have everything you need to accomplish this. Travel to the holy capital city and in the palace you shall find him. You are all we cannot be."

A loud roar erupted behind the gods. A lion the size of two human men walked toward Durga on giant paws that left indentations in the ground. When it stood before the goddess, it lay down. One of her hands brushed the fur of its head. It moved closer to her, allowing her to stroke it as it became bound to her.

She looked back to the gods and nodded, then climbed onto the back of the lion. It let out a great roar before setting off toward the capital.

Durga rode into battle with confidence. The lion's giant body leapt across the miles as it roared without tiring, fire in its eyes. When the palace came into sight, she could see Mahishasura's army gathered. The destructive nature of the asuras was apparent from the accumulated filth and fires strewn across the land. She raised her weapons, poised to strike all the demons down. Her foe had to see she did not come here for courtship or diplomacy. She had arrived to ensure Mahishasura's death.

A group of four asuras spotted her in the distance, riding toward them. They smirked as she got closer seeing she was a woman, but their amusement was cut short as her sword sliced straight through them, separating torsos from hips. Taken by surprise, the other asuras scrambled to gather their weapons, but Durga didn't pause despite their great numbers. She used every weapon at her disposal to slay the asuras before they had a chance to strike her down. Power surged in her like the rays of the sun on a hot day. It blinded her enemies and made them helpless to her attack.

Hearing the commotion, Mahishasura rushed outside the palace. He watched in disbelief as this goddess of immense light and ferocity took down his army. Severed limbs, shouts, streams of blood, roars of a lion ... his disbelief soon turned to rage. His body grew as his dark emotions gathered momentum. *No one* could defeat him. How dare the gods try!

"You! You shall die!" he snarled at Durga in a booming voice that travelled far across the land.

Durga continued her slaughter, scarcely acknowledging the demon. He blasted hot air from his nostrils and fell to the ground, letting out a strained cry as the muscles on his body thickened and brown bristles sprouted all over him. His hands turned to hooves like his feet. His head reared toward Durga. He had transformed into a giant buffalo.

Durga chopped the arms off the final asura and turned her attention to the raging buffalo. Now it was his turn to die and fulfill her mission and destiny. With eyes locked onto each other, they charged.

Ten days passed as Mahishasura shifted from the form of a buffalo to a lion, a serpent, an elephant and back to a buffalo again. All of this to evade Durga and make her lose hope. But she did not give up. Her warrior spirit and vast power would not let her.

With all the weapons gifted to her, and ten arms to protect herself, Durga finally cornered a weary Mahishasura, who had become a buffalo again. He had slowed and his breathing was more laboured than before, but this was still his most potent form. Hot eddies of breath escaped his mouth and nostrils as he composed himself for another fight with her. His eyes glowed bright red. He charged toward Durga at full speed. Dirt flew into the air, creating a storm of soil. The goddess stood her ground until he got closer. Right before he could knock her over, she deftly guided the lion out of his way and thrust the trident through his back.

Mahishasura skidded away from her. Durga jumped from the back of the lion and ran toward him. He howled as he tried to get up, but he was pinned to the ground. She pulled out the trident, causing him to howl again. Without remorse, she hacked into his meaty neck with her sword until his head separated from his body.

Durga surveyed the devastation. The palace of the gods was littered with asura appendages and pools of blood. Their demon leader now lay dead. Balance had been restored, and the gift of Shakti – divine feminine energy – was now for all to experience.

Durga – Fierce and Steadfast Warrior

The essence of the Hindu goddess Durga is that of a supreme warrior and she is revered for her fierceness when facing her demon adversaries in the various stories of her battles. She is sometimes depicted wearing bright red and as having eight to eighteen arms, each holding a symbolic object. Some of these are weapons as mentioned in the story and there are others such as the conch shell. In some stories her immense beauty is part of her power as she is the embodiment of Shakti – commanding, creative feminine energy. She is associated with protection and is a mother goddess. Durga has nine manifestations who are celebrated during her festivals:

Shailpurti: This form of Durga is the daughter of the great Himalayas. She rides a bull named Nandi and carries a lotus and a trident. Her devotees ask her for health and prosperity.

Brahmacharini: This form only has two hands. One carries a pot and the other mala beads. She represents the harmony achieved through penance and meditation. Her devotees are blessed with the ability to move through life's challenges with courage.

Chandraghanta: She is ready for war if need be, with ten hands. Some of those hold weapons and she also carries a lotus. Two of her hands are in mudras (symbolic gestures). She has a moon on her forehead. For devotees she represents courage and discipline.

Kushmanda: This form of Durga rides a tiger and is surrounded by a golden hue. She is considered the creator of the universe and can bestow abundance upon her devotees.

Skandamanta: She also rides a lion, but in one hand she carries an infant (Lord Skanda or Kartikeya) with six faces. Her other two hands carry lotus flowers. She is a mother who gives peace and frees her devotees from worry.

Katyayani: This is the warrior form of Durga who we see in the story shared earlier, who gives her devotees courage, determination and protection.

Kalaratri: The most violent and vicious form of Durga, who represents destruction. She is Kali, as seen in her tale earlier in this book, and offers her devotees strength, protection and the ability to overcome obstacles.

Mahagauri: She rides a white bull and is depicted with a very fair complexion. For her devotees, she represents spiritual transformation. Two of her hands are positioned in mudras and the others carry a trident and a drum.

Siddhidhatri: The final form of Durga sits on a lotus and blesses her devotees with knowledge, spirituality and wisdom.

Durga is celebrated during the nine-day Indian festival of Navratri. In some parts of India, Navratri coincides with Durga Puja, a large-scale celebration of her victory over the demon Mahishasura as described in this tale.

The original source for the story told here is the Devi Mahatmya in the Markandeya Purana, and Durga is also mentioned in the Rigveda and Atharvaveda. In Mamallapuram in Tamil Nadu, India, the legend has been carved into a panel in the ancient rock-cut cave temple Mahishasuramardini Mandapa.

Durga Wisdom

You already have everything you need to succeed and overcome any obstacles in your way. These are innate qualities that no one can give to you or take away from you. Like Durga, remain as steadfast to your purpose as the sun in the heavens, which never wanes in intensity. Anything that disrupts the sun's greatness is like cloud or smoke, which always eventually passes. The sun itself remains undimmed.

Athena

A Grave Challenge

Arachne's bench was a fallen tree trunk. It was in the perfect position between shade from other trees and the warm sun. She sat there thinking about what she would weave next. Her fingers touched the thread and she smiled. She was known far and wide for her beautiful designs and creations. People travelled to her home in Lydia just to watch her at work. There was really no one better than her at weaving, if she could say so herself. It gave her great pride to be known for this gift that no one else seemed to have, not even the gods themselves.

An old woman huddled in a cape approached her. Her back was hunched over and loose strands of white hair fell from the hood that shaded her face. The clothes she wore were simple and threadbare. "You have great skill. It must come from the gods. Athena herself must have bestowed this gift on you."

Arachne gave the old woman a disgusted look. "What silliness are you talking about? This is *my* talent. I would like Athena herself to try to do a better job than me. If she ever dared to show her face. The gods just sit around and do nothing, except expect us to pray to them."

"Surely you don't mean that. Ask forgiveness for this blasphemy," said the old woman in a soft voice. She reached out to touch Arachne's work, an intricate image of a bouquet of flowers. The young woman snatched the cloth away with a look of disdain and irritation.

"Only if she can do a better job than me. Let her come down and try." Arachne turned her back on the old woman.

The old woman ripped off her cape and threw back her hair, now more gold than white. She was no longer feeble and small. Her upright posture made her impossibly tall and her face was an elegant picture of beauty. It was Athena herself.

"I heard rumours of a young mortal bragging about her weaving skills and I had to see for myself."

Athena stood yet taller and glowed in the sunlight as she stared down on Arachne, expecting the young woman to humble herself instantly. "You do not have to look any further or boast any longer. I am here and I accept your challenge." The goddess held in her hand all she needed to weave a great tapestry.

Arachne laughed and kept her cool even in the presence of a goddess. She didn't bother to rise to her feet or bow her head out of respect. "Fine. I am not afraid of you."

They began the weaving competition. Athena created a tapestry displaying all the gods in triumphant glory during their adventures. Her hands moved swiftly, her expertise truly divine. Craft was one of her special domains, after all, and countless humans touched by her creative inspiration had given her thanks and praise.

It wasn't long until she had completed her piece. Arachne studied it then got to work on her own, which, however, was not as complimentary to the gods. She created scenes showing the gods in compromising positions with each other and humans. As her fingers moved seemingly of their own accord, she chuckled to herself as she created scandalous details that made the deities look like fools. Athena watched with intensity as the picture became more clear.

When she finished, Arachne held it up. "What do you think of mine?" Her confidence and the look of gloating on her face enraged Athena. She couldn't believe the gall of this human. How she mocked the gods! But her skill was undeniable – there wasn't a single flaw.

Athena flew into a rage. With her shuttle and all her strength, she began to beat Arachne. "How dare you!" she shouted at the young woman. Her blows continued until Arachne was on the ground, begging her to stop.

But Athena didn't stop until all her contempt had been released. She looked upon Arachne with smug satisfaction. Bright welts had formed on her skin. The young woman's shoulders heaved as she cried.

"Serves you right. Don't ever think you can speak like that again about one so above you. Pitiful human, you will die with this memory," Athena said in a spiteful tone, before turning to leave.

Arachne wept on her knees, her dress torn and body bruised. Her cut lip dripped blood onto her thigh which was turning different shades of purple and blue. After this humiliation by a goddess, how could she ever show her face again? Her body ached as she rose to her feet. The only way she could go on was to pass from this realm.

From the barn behind her parents' house, she gathered rope and a stool. Then she went to the great olive tree that she had loved to sit beneath as a child. It was where she had perfected her craft. The craft that had now brought shame upon her and her family. Every step took her closer to her fate until she stood next to the olive tree. She tossed the rope over a branch and created a noose. Without a letter or any goodbyes to her loved ones, she placed her neck within the loop and thrust herself from the stool.

Her legs swung back and forth, then they stopped. Athena's hand curled around her ankle. She had only wanted to teach the haughty human a lesson. The girl could never be human again, but Athena could do something else for her. Arachne's vibrant talent would not be lost, and she could still do what she loved.

Athena pulled the noose from the tree. As Arachne's body crumpled to the ground, she began to shrink and change into the shape of a spider. The rope also shrank and became a long, silky thread attached to the transformed Arachne.

Athena kneeled down and took the spider into her hand. "Go forth and create. Let it be your purpose and may it bring you joy."

Athena – Protector with a Wrathful Streak

You will recognize the face on Athena's aegis (shield), because it is the head of Medusa. To protect herself, Athena also wears full armour and carries a spear. An owl is also always nearby. Sometimes she is seen with a snake.

This all makes sense considering she is the Greek goddess of war, handicrafts and wisdom. To the Romans, she was Minerva (and in this form she appears in the story of Medusa earlier in this book). Her parents were the mighty Zeus and Metis, which makes her an Olympian – an immortal goddess with immense power. She is said to have sprung out of Zeus's head after he swallowed her mother whole when a prophecy stated their child would want to take his place. She climbed out of Zeus's split head as a full-grown adult, dressed for battle.

Athena's attributes make her a formidable ally and she has helped many heroes on their quests through Greek and Roman mythology. However, as seen here and in the story of Medusa, she wasn't always the most benevolent. The tale of Athena and Arachne was recounted by the Roman poet Ovid in *Metamorphoses*, a source also for the legends of Medusa and Hecate. Athena is also featured in Homer's great works, the *Iliad* and the *Odyssey*.

Athena's most important place of worship is Athens. She is the patron of this city and the great Parthenon is dedicated to her. In one of her tales, she had to challenge Poseidon for this honour. She offered the city the olive tree and he offered sea dominance. The people chose Athena's gift. She is also credited for giving humankind the chariot, the ship, the plough and pottery.

Athena Wisdom

If you must go to war, do not let it be with yourself or with one who could scarcely defend themselves against you. If you find yourself in a place of privilege, then choose to use it in a constructive way. The ego wants to outshine others, but the divine dark feminine doesn't need to flex to prove she is better than someone else. Doing so comes from insecurity and a sense of lack.

Athena also teaches that lies, name calling, unwarranted discrediting and other negative actions come with consequences. The divine dark feminine wields her power with grace and discernment.

Mictecacihuatl

Death and Rebirth in Mictlan

The infant girl squirmed in the arms of the priestess chanting prayers over the child. The baby's cries echoed through the fire and incense of this autumn equinox night. The child's mother did not survive the birth and had no chance to welcome her daughter with a loving glance or kiss. She would travel to a place where other brave mothers who passed in childbirth dwelled. She would be honoured. She would never know that her daughter would become greater in death than she ever would in life. In her death, her purpose would be found.

The priestess lifted the infant overhead with tears in her eyes. Drums pounded in the distance. Someone blew the conch shell. The priestess tossed the infant into the cenote, the water-filled sinkhole through which she would travel from life to death and back to life again in another form. The baby's little lungs filled with water. A whirlpool formed, sucking her to the depths as she passed to her new home.

In Mictlan, the nine-levelled Aztec underworld, she would outgrow her skin until it fell off, leaving only muscle, blood and bone. Her sacrifice as a human was nothing compared to what she would gain: she would reign over the nine trials of the dead as they journeyed to reveal their tonalli, their soul energy, should they make it through. That nameless child from a dead mother would be queen.

This is the death and rebirth of Mictēcacihuātl. Her holy presence is everywhere in Mictlan, but one must prove oneself worthy to reach her and find the peace the dead seek.

Esperanza Salinas exhaled her final breath surrounded by her loved ones, then allowed her double vision to tunnel until there was only the dark embrace of nothingness. But now she found herself standing alone on the wooded bank of a river.

"Are you ready for your next journey? It is perilous, but you can make it if you want to."

She turned around and gasped. Before her stood a woman without skin or flesh. The muscles on her body dripped with blood. Her eye sockets were black wells. She wore a headdress made from multicoloured feathers and a necklace of large beads of jade.

Esperanza knew exactly who this was. It was the Aztec queen of the dead, Mictēcacihuātl.

"My lady, I am but an old woman."

"Are you?"

Esperanza looked down. Her body had become young again. "I don't understand."

"I will watch as you make your way to the place where your spirit can experience true peace. Show me you are worthy of help."

The queen walked to Esperanza and touched her forehead, leaving a red fingerprint. In that instant, Esperanza knew exactly how the dead could move through all levels of Mictlan.

She was in the first level, Chiconahuapan. A rushing river separated her from where she needed to be. A dog, a Mexican hairless xoloitzcuintle, came bounding through the trees, its large, pointed ears twitching. It stopped in front of Esperanza and regarded her with a questioning air, as if sensing how kind she had been to dogs in her life.

"I had a dog named Ganas when I was little. I loved that little terrier. Please help me."

The hound gave Esperanza a friendly lick, then jumped into the raging torrent and guided her across. She looked back but the goddess was gone.

She was now in level two, or Tepectli Monamictlán, where two mountains rose and fell in sync, smashing into each other as they did so. The atmosphere was filled with clouds of dust and flying rubble. The ground shook with the violence of an earthquake. Esperanza had to make her way between the two mountains without being crushed. If she succeeded, there was a third mountain and a third level – Iztepetl. The ground here was strewn with jagged shards of flint and rock. One false move and her body would be shredded to ribbons. Even if she avoided a fatal stumble and fall, her feet would not go unscathed. She would have to endure the path of painful steps.

Esperanza looked up to the mountains and saw the Mictēcacihuātl standing on a peak. "If you focus on being crushed, then you will be crushed. No life is without pain. But can you experience such pain and still go forward?" Her voiced boomed through the purple and pink-streaked sky.

Esperanza swallowed hard. She knew pain. She knew joy. And she also knew what was required to persevere. She looked at the mountains gnashing like teeth. With determination, she ran through a gap. When the rocks underfoot became as sharp as broken glass, she slowed and watched her steps, taking a deep breath whenever a shard pierced her skin. There was no rush. She just had to make it through. And she did.

Now the temperature was dropping. Her teeth chattered and her arms had turned to gooseflesh. Her hair flew in all directions in the howling wind as the voice of the goddess whispered in her ear.

"Welcome to the other side of the mountains. This is the place of frigid winds, or level four, Itzehecayan. In this snowy valley, the icy wind will cut like obsidian arrows. Are you brave enough to move forward? And can you surrender to what you can't control and let yourself fly? Remember that the spirit is pliable and moves as such."

The voice stopped and so did Esperanza, for just a moment, as the wind lashed her face and body. The harsh and unrelenting weather had to be navigated without pausing or turning back. Just as she'd done on the path of painful steps, she put one foot in front of the other and slowly moved forward, hugging her arms to try to stay warm. She tried to focus on the good times in her life and the things that had made her laugh. Anything to keep her going, because from what Mictēcacihuātl said, there was more to come.

Just when she thought she was making progress, the wind picked up again for level five, Paniecatoyan. Here, the winds actually lifted her off her feet, blowing her to and fro in every direction, as if gravity did not exist. Esperanza did her best not to resist. The only way to get through this level was to endure until the wind dumped her back on the ground. It felt like her body was being torn in half. Her eyes searched for the goddess, but she was nowhere to be seen.

A twister pulled her so high she could see the top of the mountain. A moon glittered brightly. She smiled at the sight then dropped in the span of seconds. Just before she hit the ground at full speed, her feet touched down with the softness of a floating feather. Ahead of her was a calm, wide path with dense woods on either side. No moving mountains, tornados or anything else to disrupt her journey. It appeared easy, but she knew it couldn't be.

The goddess appeared from behind a large boulder. "Congratulations. You are still standing. On this level, Timiminaloayan, all things lost are found again. The arrows that lay embedded in the dead are here given new life."

"There is more pain to come?"

"Like regret, the arrows will only pierce you if you let them."

Esperanza wanted to ask her more, but the goddess clasped her hands and disappeared behind the boulder.

So it was the trees she had to worry about. She took a deep breath and began to sprint down the path.

One by one, arrows whizzed through the air to stop her. The assailants were unseen, and the arrows took on a life of their own. When they nicked and pierced her body she screamed, but she knew that is what they were meant to do. Cause discouragement, fear and panic. She kept running as the arrows zoomed around her. She pumped her arms harder as her surroundings began to change, the path now crowded with bigger, wilder trees making a high canopy and dense undergrowth. The humidity increased. The arrows stopped and the path led into the darkness of a tropical jungle. Esperanza's heart was beating fast from sprinting, but also from fearing the test that awaited her inside.

The trees above her rustled. The goddess sat on a thick branch with a python around her neck, its small head resting on her lap. She stroked its head as it licked her bloody torso.

"You have been led to Teocoyohuehualoyan, the wild jungle of level seven. Shadows will stalk you like hungry creatures. In the green darkness lurk the fiercest of foes, the jaguars. They will watch you with yellow eyes, fang and claw, waiting to rip the hearts from those who pass through. Can you tame the beast within?"

"I can try," said Esperanza.

The goddess gave her a smile. "Maybe that is all that is required. Now go."

The parted foliage covered her again. Esperanza looked at the jungle pressing in all around her. Jaguars. They were beautiful and ferocious like the goddess herself. Esperanza closed her eyes and imagined herself as a jaguar. Then she opened her eyes and began to walk forward as if she too were part of the jungle.

Tangled trees and thick undergrowth blotted out the sun. It had become very hot. The sounds of birds, monkeys and insects surrounded her. She walked slowly and calmed her racing heart. Out of the corner of her eye, she glimpsed two eyes shining through the brush. She stopped and looked directly into them. For a moment she held the unseen beast's gaze and gave it a nod of respect before continuing on. She heard a hiss then branches breaking as something moved away.

More light was breaking through the canopy and now the trees thinned to reveal a dark lake. Esperanza thought it looked as black and shiny as obsidian that you could walk across.

"But you cannot walk across it," boomed the goddess's voice. The feathers of her headdress rose from the dark water, then her head. As she floated above Esperanza, black droplets like crude oil fell from her body.

"Now, my dear, you must traverse the black lagoon of level eight, Izmictlan Apochacalolca. It is time to shed all that ties you to the old you, and to your old world, so you may explore the new. Only your spirit will remain. You are close now to true liberation. After you have crossed the lagoon, there is only one final test and it would be a pity to fail then. You will reach level nine, Chicunamictlan. It is the cleansing before we meet again."

Liberation. Emotional and mental freedom. Enlightenment. Esperanza could feel she was so close. But it meant leaving behind the mortal version of her. Letting her loved ones become a distant memory of a life already lived.

Slowly, she waded into the darkness of the water, the goddess watching overhead. As she swam farther, flakes of skin floated to the water's surface. She could see patches of her flesh peeling away. It didn't hurt. In fact, there was a buoyancy in her body. She swam faster and more of her body floated away. And she let it go. She surrendered to being physically dismantled so that the real Esperanza could emerge.

When she reached the other side of the lagoon, she could see there were more lakes that she had to pass through. She touched her exposed muscles that were dripping with blood and black water. It was time. Time to move on.

In this new state without skin, just bloody muscle, she found her way through thick, disorienting fog and crossed nine more lagoons to cleanse and free herself completely from the remnants of her old life. Without trying, she contemplated her human existence, deeds and thoughts. Now, chunks of muscle floated from her and fish rose to carry her body away. It didn't matter. There was no pain, only acceptance. Her bones glittered, iridescent.

She stepped from the waters in a liberated state of consciousness. On the bank, the queen of the dead extended her hand to her. Hunger, pain, worry and all the ties of life were gone.

"Well done. You have completed your journey. Come with me now and you shall exist in peace."

Esperanza was ready.

Mictēcacihuātl – Death is Only the Start for Her

She is the goddess of the multi-level underworld Mictlan described here. Most people who died of old age or natural causes found themselves here after death. However, Mictlan was only one underworld. If you were a woman who died in childbirth, for example, you would go to a different underworld.

Mictēcacihuātl and her husband, Mictlāntēcutli, help human souls traverse the trials of the nine levels of the underworld. They are also the keepers of the bones of the dead. The feathered serpent god Quetzalcoatl wanted to use the bones to create new humans. He tried to steal them without Mictēcacihuātl and Mictlāntēcutli's knowledge after they denied his request. Mictlāntēcutl dug a hole in the ground to trap Quetzalcoatl and sure enough he fell into the hole along with the bones he had stolen. They were jumbled up and broken, but he didn't mind. He escaped the hole and returned above ground. There, the bones were ground into a paste and mixed with the blood of the gods to create more humans.

Mictēcacihuātl's appearance is terrifying as she has no skin and looks like a bloody skeleton. There are some statues of her in museums in Mexico and there is an image in the Codex Borgia, which was created by the Aztecs and survived the conquest.

To find out more about Mictlan and Mictēcacihuātl, you can read the *Florentine Codex*, *Codex Ramírez* or *Codex Vaticanus A-Ríos*, although it is important to bear in mind the inherent bias of these texts. Written by the Spanish when they encountered the Indigenous population, they represent records made by Christians who didn't fully understand the culture or practices they were describing, and whose intention was to convert and assimilate.

Mictecacihuatl Wisdom

You can face life's trials with a spirit of defeat or you can approach them determined to meet a stronger version of yourself. Sometimes life can feel like hell as we endure problem after problem with no end in sight. We may wonder if we are alone or if there is anyone to guide and help us. Rise to the challenges like the one who has everything to gain and nothing to lose. Rise to claim your throne like the goddess Mictēcacihuātl, who had to journey through the deep waters of the cenote to be reborn as queen of the dead. Wisdom, fortitude and the deepening of self-understanding are all great gifts that await you.

OSHUN

The Divinity of Abundance

Olodumare created the world, but it was incomplete. There was a void, a lack of softness; a flow of feminine energy was needed to nurture the beautiful aspects of his creation.

"Seventeen orishas I will send down. The final orisha, my sacred and precious Oshun, will be the last but most important part of my creation," he said to himself.

The male orishas plotted and shouted over one another as they tried to follow Olodumare's instructions to finish populating the Earth. Oshun listened and watched. Their arguments over which way was best ran in circles. Not one of them looked in her direction even though she had been sent with them as their equal. She attempted to step forward, but two orishas blocked her way as they argued. Their bodies created an impenetrable barrier she had no desire to fight her way through.

Oshun shook her head in frustration and left. She was obviously not wanted. There was a riverbank nearby where the saplings needed nurturing and looking after, to grow into the beautiful shade trees she knew they could be. Oshun made herself comfortable and imagined all the potential life the river and its bank could create. The fish jumped from the water. Birds dove into the river and flew back out with a meal in their beaks. All manner of insects swarmed around her in a cacophony of natural song. Grass sprouted from the rich soil and fat earthworms squirmed beneath the surface. The saplings became mature trees that provided ample protection from sun or rain. Bees buzzed around a branch and encased it in honeycomb. Sweet nectar fell upon Oshun's shoulder. She touched it and tasted it. The sweetness pleased her tongue. It made her smile.

A peacock lay down next to her and allowed some of its ornate feathers to fall into her lap. "I shall make a beautiful fan from your gift, thank you," she said.

Oshun smiled and felt her divine energy continue to create beauty and joy. And the entire time she didn't hear a word from the other orishas.

"This cannot be!" shouted Shango. "We have tried all our ideas and yet the ground is still barren, the animals weak and small. We must go back to Olodumare and tell him something is not right."

The orishas nodded in agreement. Exhausted and frustrated, they wanted to give up on this impossible task.

They made a tight circle, each invoking the name of Olodumare until his presence could be felt.

"Why have you called upon me? And how is your progress? Show me what you have done."

"We have achieved nothing," said Shango. "You have set us up to fail in this task."

There was a silence. "I did not. Everything was as it should be ... And where is Oshun? I do not see her, yet she was sent into the world with you."

The orishas looked around. No one had noticed her absence. "We don't know. We didn't speak to her. We were too busy planning solutions for the problem of this place."

"Problem? This is not a riddle to be solved or a game to win. This realm I have created is intended to be *experienced*, in all its aspects. That is why I sent Oshun. Her heart, her very essence is in this experience, and it is her essence that you need."

The orishas were dumbfounded and shamed by their own ignorance.

"Go find her. Follow the sounds of life. You must not exclude her or there will be consequences, as you have already seen."

Olodumare said no more. He retreated into the heavy meditation of infinite omniscience.

"Follow the sounds of life ... can any of you hear what life is?" asked Shango.

They stood in silence, but nothing could be heard until a hummingbird flew above their heads. It flitted playfully but with immense strength. "We follow that!" said one of the orishas.

The journey through barren land and barely trickling creeks soon led to lush green pastures and fruit-bearing trees. The orishas looked on in wonder. Beneath a tree sat Oshun, enjoying the warmth of the sunshine and holding a fan made from peacock feathers. She was surrounded by an abundance of thriving life. The brightness of the sun cast a golden hue around her.

Shango approached her. "You left us."

She looked up. "You acted as if you didn't need me, as if I had nothing of value to offer. Why would I stay?"

He kneeled, as it was apparent she would not rise to her feet to speak to him. "On behalf of us all: we are very sorry. We were wrong. Please show us how you achieved all of this. How long did it take you? Was it difficult? How did you force these living things to obey your will and grow so fast?"

She chuckled. "You are seeing it all wrong. You do not force life; you allow it to flow like this river. Those bees made this honey because they wanted to. It is why they were created. Everything you see here has its own place and works with everything else. Doing less can sometimes mean gaining more. Appreciating what already exists will allow it to bloom more than you can imagine."

He looked upon her with reverence. "Then we shall do it your way. Please help us and be a guide to bring the earth to its fullest potential."

She fanned herself and gave him a confident, somewhat sultry smile. "I will, because I can."

Oshun – Sweetness and Spite

Oshun is the youngest orisha from the Yoruba religion of West Africa. She is the sister (some say daughter) of Yemaya, the orisha who represents the oceans, and partner to Shango, the orisha of thunder.

Like Yemaya (whose legend is also told in this book), Oshun is associated with flowing water (in Oshun's case, sweet or freshwater rivers and streams), and she is also the goddess of love, fertility, beauty, sensuality, pleasure, joy, attraction, harmony and abundance. The world is sweet and overflowing because of her. She is shown carrying a mirror to admire her beauty and yellow or gold is her favourite colour. Other symbols linked to her include a fan of peacock feathers, a pot of honey tied around her waist and gold jewellery.

But do not think she cannot feel anger or cause floods and droughts if she is not appeased by devotees. In another tale we also see the extent of her jealousy and spite. Oshun is married to Shango but is his second wife. Oba is the first and is considered the legitimate spouse. He also had a third wife named Oya. On one occasion, Oba prepared yam porridge for her husband. Oshun said that Shango would love Oba more if she showed her devotion with a sacrifice. She urged her to cut off her ear and serve it to him. Oba did just that. When Shango discovered the ear, he raged and sent Oba away. She left heartbroken and transformed into the River Oba. Oshun was not spared his anger and she too fled and transformed into her own river.

At the Osun-Osogbo Sacred Grove in the forest on the outskirts of Osogbo in Nigeria, you can find many shrines dedicated to Oshun, because this is where she first had contact with humans and allowed the people to worship her and build a town. She is also the protector of Nigeria's River Oshun. Every August she is celebrated at the12-day Osun-Osogbo festival, which has been taking place for hundreds of years and is still a huge attraction.

Believers come to Oshun seeking love, prosperity and fertility. For offerings, the colour yellow is significant. She likes honey, oranges, pumpkins and yellow flowers (sunflowers are a favourite). Peacock feathers can be placed on an altar for her, too.

Oshun is also venerated in Cuban Santería, Brazilian Candomblé and Haitian Vodou. A book I can personally recommend about Oshun and Santería is *Santería: The Religion* by Migene González-Wippler.

Oshun Wisdom

Creativity is divine. Always pay attention to your inner sparks of intuitive creation. It is easy to dismiss our creative passions as something that should take a back seat to more practical things in life. Maybe you yearn to write a book, or take up painting or to pursue something else not traditionally considered lucrative. Oshun teaches us that it is okay to stop thinking that creativity has no place in the "real world". In this story she was dismissed and ignored as the other gods toiled and debated the logistics of building a world. She quietly walked away and created life anyway. Give yourself the freedom to fan your creative flames.

Yemaya – Yoruba

(West Africa)

The Waters of Creation

The universe was a vast womb that had given birth to many mysteries over an infinity of time and space. One of the unseen dimensions was Orun. This is where the orishas resided before the creation of humanity. And this is where Olodumare, the greatest of all energies, presided over eternity with his omniscient consciousness.

"It is time, Yemaya, Mother of Fish," a deep voice whispered to her. It was Olodumare.

"Yes, I feel myself growing heavier."

"You must join Obotala in a new creation – humans."

She bowed her head in reverence. "And how should we do this, Wise One?"

Before her eyes, a long rope of stardust and nebulous gas began to twist in the atmosphere. It gave off a dim glow as it grew thicker with each twist, making it strong enough to carry the weight of the orishas. "You shall join the other orishas to journey to Aye – Earth. There you shall become a mother again."

Yemaya touched her belly and then the rope. It felt sturdy, yet soft to the touch. She nestled one foot inside a loop hanging from the cosmic pulley. When both her feet were secure, it began to move in a downward spiral. She travelled past Orun and through the vast darkness of the universe toward the emerald-coloured gem called Earth.

She passed the moon, admiring its cool white light as it shone in its full glory. She continued to descend until she stood on Earth's soil with her bare feet. The muscles below her belly tightened and spasmed. The journey was not long, but long enough for her to know she would not remain pregnant through the night. The moon would witness this birth, and its light would guide her. She found a flat piece of land suitable for giving birth. The ache within her belly became deeper and the cramps more acute. She knew she held inside her a new beginning that only she could conceive and bring forth. Divine energy tumbled and churned within her.

Glistening water trickled from between her legs. The pool was like a mirror in the moonlight. She leaned back on her hands to allow her body to do what it instinctively must do. Water continued to flow as her body opened to this new world. Soon the water was surging in all directions, carving stretchmarks into the soil and filling them. She glanced down to see that a river had formed at her feet. "Ogun. You shall be called the River Ogun," she whispered. She closed her eyes and allowed more life-giving liquid to gush from her body. The moonlight pulled on the great seas sloshing between her ankles as she squeezed her eyes shut to push out what remained inside. It wouldn't be long until the birth was complete. The waters rushed over the land and settled across the entire planet. She fell onto her back with her belly empty. In the distance, the first light of the sun could be seen. She smiled and sat upright to see her creation.

"Thank you, Great Mother." It was Olodumare speaking to her again.

"I shall look after those who call on me by the mighty bodies of water and leave offerings with their petitions," Yemaya replied. "My love will extend to mothers who feel their waters break and their children crowning. All who come to be in love will receive my love in return, as a child is loved by their mother."

Yemaya – Mother of All

Also called Yemoja, Yemaya is an orisha originally venerated by the Yoruba people of West Africa. Quintessentially African, she was first associated with the River Ogun of Nigeria until she crossed the ocean with the African diaspora and is now venerated in various belief systems across the Americas. On New Year's Day in Brazil, for example, many throw white flowers into the ocean as an offering to her. Water is her domain, specifically saltwater (freshwater rivers and streams belong to the other Yoruba goddess featured in this book, Oshun). We sometimes see Yemaya depicted as a beautiful mermaid or a woman in a flowing gown that melts into waves as she floats on the ocean.

Many consider her a calming and loving deity, but very protective of those who venerate her. She is the carer of mothers and pregnant women, looking after children and amniotic fluid, and also assisting with fertility. Her fierceness can be attributed to turbulent rivers or seas. Those who work in water or who travel on water find protection with her. It is important to note, however, that Yemaya dwells on the surface of the ocean and it is another orisha, Olokin, who has dominion over the sea's darkest depths.

This is just one version of Yemaya's story. There is a darker tale steeped in pain and horror, which tells how Yemaya was raped by her own son. After this indignity, she fled to a mountaintop in grief and shame. She cursed her son until he died. Unable to recover, she took her own life. As she died, her waters broke and her breasts leaked, creating water on the Earth as well as fourteen orishas. Humans also sprang forth from her body.

Much of what we know of the orishas has been handed down through the oral tradition, and colonization and enslavement impacted how these stories were preserved, told and changed. The rituals involved in veneration also differ from place to place. In the African diaspora, the tales evolved over time depending on location and the mixing of cultures and religions. Yemaya is associated with cowrie shells (used as a tool for divination), the number seven, the moon (as it pertains to the tides) and the colours blue and white.

You can walk into most botànicas (specialist spiritual shops in the Americas) and find pillar candles dedicated to Yemaya, typically with her image in blue and a prayer or blessing written on the back. She looks peaceful and beautiful on these candles as she floats above the water, her open arms ready to embrace anyone who comes to her in the correct way.

If you go to the beach and happen to find watermelon or roses, please be respectful and leave them alone. These offerings have been left by a devotee for Yemaya and Yemaya alone.

Yemaya Wisdom

To look after yourself is to love yourself. Yemaya is a nurturing and healing energy we can turn to in times of turbulence. There is a reason so many sleep and anti-anxiety apps use the hypnotic sound of waves, rain or rushing or trickling water. The sound of water can bring a real sense of tranquility and be profoundly grounding. We cannot live without water. Our ancestors settled in places where fresh water could be found, and often by the sea where they could fish. Water is life and as primal as fire.

Next time you find yourself by the sea or another large body of water, take a deep breath and exhale any troubles or challenges. Even just taking a long hot bath can be deeply relaxing, enveloping you in soothing warmth.

Yemaya reminds us that life can rock us to our core, but like a storm at sea, these choppy waters never last long. The clouds will part, and calm will return.

Yuki Onna

Phantom Beauty

The frozen winter and biting, frigid winds are her domain. She hides among the trees at the foot of snow-covered mountains, waiting for a weary lost soul to pass by. When they are completely helpless, shivering in the whiteout, that is when she makes herself known. A phantom ten feet tall, with skin as smooth as an icy lake. Her glowing violet eyes pierce and charm her prey, while her silky black hair floats around her body like dark ribbons or rope to bind them. Her beauty is undeniable, but so is her lethal embrace in which she freezes her victims with her breath.

Two loggers, Minokichi and Mosakui, trudged through the soft white powder, their hands protecting their faces from gales of snow striking their skin like shards of glass. Their feet sank until the snow reached their knees. They could barely hear each other over the howling winds.

When they finally arrived at the river they had to cross to get home, there was no ferry in sight. Their faces fell. Mosakui was shivering uncontrollably; he was seventy years old and could not go on much longer.

"Over there!" shouted Minokichi, who had better vision than his companion. He'd spotted the ferryman's hut a short distance away. It wouldn't be much, but at least they could survive the night.

They made their way to the hut. Inside, they looked for a fireplace. "I think we should just rest. I don't have the energy for anything else. At least we are away from the wind and snow," said an exhausted Mosakui, who lay down on a mat and used his satchel as a pillow.

"Yes, I think you are right." Minokichi looked out the window at the whirling snowstorm, grateful to be inside.

It didn't take long for the old man to fall asleep, his arms wrapped tight around his body. He began to snore. Minokichi did the same, trying to keep warm as he lay on the ground. But the cold kept him awake and he couldn't drift off to sleep.

A creak made him open his eyes. He wondered if he was dreaming, or having a nightmare. Through the window, which was now open, floated a luminous white figure. She was a woman as beautiful as a sunrise across a snowy valley. Her frosty skin glittered beneath luxurious black hair. Her lips were like a drop of blood on the snow. He was too afraid to move so he watched through eyes narrowed to thin slits. She hovered above the old man as he snored. Her long, wispy, black hair moved over his face and body like fingertips. Then she floated closer, until her face rested above his. With an unhinged mouth that grew to twice its size, she sucked the air out of his mouth and nostrils.

His body shrivelled with each breath she took and he froze from the top of his head to his toes. When the old man's eyeballs fell back into their sockets, Minokichi gasped, unable to contain his fright. The woman glanced up and fixed her violet eyes on him. Moving closer, she studied his face and body. In a raspy voice like cracking ice, she spoke. "Where are you from?"

"The village just across the river. The storm made us take shelter here," he stammered.

She moved yet closer. He shivered, feeling the chill of her presence nearing. "I will let you live but if you ever speak of this to anyone, then I will find you and take your life as I took his."

His teeth chattered from the cold and fear as he spoke. "Yes, I promise."

Her violet eyes glided across his body once more, then met his gaze again. "Good. Now close your eyes as I leave."

He immediately lay back down and squeezed his eyes shut. He felt conflicted by her beauty, and the terror he felt, and having to lie about how his companion had died. For the rest of the night he lay awake, wanting to face neither the dead body nor the enchanting spectre.

The ferryman returned to the hut in the morning to see Minokichi dragging his dead friend out of the hut. "Please help. We got caught in the storm last night and he didn't survive. I must get him back to his family."

The ferryman nodded, devastated by the news. "Of course, I will help. The storm was terrible and it is worse to now also know that Mosakui is dead. He travelled on my boat many times."

Minokichi and the ferryman returned the body to Mosakui's family and left them to grieve. Minokichi returned to his mother's house shivering with fever and never spoke of that night or the terrifying woman. In fits of delirium he dreamed of the ghost, wondering when he regained his senses if it had ever been real. At times he would wake up and look out his window and see her face peering in. When he sprung upright, there would only be frost on the pane. He would lie back down and try to sleep again.

The following winter, Minokichi walked through the forest with a bundle of wood toward the ferry. He noticed a young woman waiting by the river. She was taller than him and striking, with large black eyes and long black hair. He couldn't take his eyes off her and felt strangely compelled to speak to her. "Hello, I've not seen you before. I am Minokichi."

She smiled. "Both my parents have died and I must travel to Yedo to stay with my aunt. She will help me to find work. My name is O-Yuki." Her voice was as delicate as a flute.

"What a wonderful name. It suits you because you are as beautiful as a morning of fresh snow."

She blushed at his comment. The ferry neared. Minokichi asked, "May I keep you company for now? I will help you with your bag."

The pink of her cheeks and lips made him think of cherry blossoms in the spring.

"Yes, I would like that." She handed him her bag.

On the ferry, they sat side by side. Even though they didn't speak, Minokichi could not stop staring at the girl's skin and trying to catch her glances. His heart pounded the closer they got to the opposite side of the river. He knew he had to do something lest she slip away from him forever. Love had struck him at first sight.

When they disembarked, he extended his hand to help her off the boat. "If you are tired and hungry, would you like to visit my home to share a humble meal with my mother? I am sure she wouldn't mind the company. She always makes more than enough food."

O-Yuki smiled. "If it will not be a problem for your mother, I would be glad to rest. I have been travelling for some time."

"Yes, I insist."

His mother was surprised when she saw the young woman. "My son, welcome home. And who is this?"

"This is O-Yuki. She is travelling to Yedo and I invited her to rest for a bit."

His mother seemed just as taken with the young woman as he. She often talked about finding a matchmaker for him. "She is most welcome. Please sit."

The mother served O-Yuki and Minokichi tea while dinner cooked. "May I ask dear, are you betrothed?" she said.

"No, I am not."

The old woman smiled. "Neither is my son! I cannot wait to have grandchildren."

The three talked until dark. Instead of O-Yuki leaving that evening, she stayed. And, as fate would have it, she never made it to Yedo.

The years went by after O-Yuki and Minokichi got married. His mother enjoyed five of their ten children, as she passed away before seeing the birth of them all. However, as Minokichi found himself ageing, his wife seemed to be perpetually young and beautiful. She looked to him just as she did the day they met.

One night a snowstorm blew into the village. While the children slept and O-Yuki sat on a chair sewing, Minokichi looked out the window in deep thought.

"Why are you over there and so quiet?" she asked.

"This storm brings back memories."

She didn't look up. "Of what, my love? Tell me."

He hesitated at first. "I only say this because you are the love of my life and this storm and your timeless beauty remind me of another woman I met before. But, unlike you, she frightened me to my core."

"And?"

He told her the entire story of that dreadful night. When he had finished, she looked up at last and threw down her sewing. Her hair unravelled from her bun and began to grow, falling to her feet in a wild, dark cascade. Her eyes glowed with violet rage. She was now ten feet tall. "You promised me you would never speak of that night! Look what you have done! You have ruined everything!"

Her look of fury turned to a bitter wind. Frosty tears ran down her cheeks, then shattered as broken ice on the floor.

Minokichi cowered before the ghost. "I am sorry! I didn't know. I only told you out of my love for you."

She swooped toward him. "I will spare your life because of our beautiful children. Your punishment is to lose me forever."

She slowly faded to a cloud of snow that burst through the window and melted into the storm. Heartbroken Minokichi ran to the window, reaching for his wife who had fled. His heart and soul had become a barren place of regret and the pain was worse than any slow death in a blizzard.

Yuki Onna – Icy Succubus

Yuki Onna is a yōkai, one of many Japanese supernatural entities, ghosts and monsters. This is one of the saddest yet most frightening of Japanese stories because of the ghost's human aspects.

As with many folktales, the legend varies from region to region. In some versions she is a human who died in the snow and continues to haunt the location, while in other stories she is an evil phantom living off the life force of humans whose breath she sucks.

The first written account of Yuki Onna, by a monk who claimed to have seen her, dates to the fourteenth century. But as with most folktales, the story could go back much further than this. The tale recounted here is based on a 1904 retelling by Lafcadio Hearn, a writer and translator who introduced Japanese stories to the English-speaking world.

Today you can find Yuki Onna as an anime character in the manga series *YuYu Hakusho* and portrayed in films such as *The Snow Woman* (1968) and *Yuki Onna* (2016).

Yuki Onna Wisdom

No one is immune to loneliness. It is okay to admit to wanting some warm companionship for the cold seasons of life. Yuki Onna left her life of stalking humans to become one herself and create a family. However, she did this after asking her desired partner to not betray her. When that trust was broken, she revealed herself and fled.

Trust is as delicate as a snowflake. A single touch can make it vanish forever. When you make a promise of love and fidelity, keep it.

Freyja

The Currency of Desire

The goddess Freyja wandered past a lively village and into the forest to enjoy the last of the autumnal light. The trees were changing from deep green to gold and amber. A slight chill could be felt and the scent of burning wood from lit hearths filled the air. Leaves brushed against the hem of her cream gown as she walked along the path.

Through the open door and window of a stone hut, she saw two dwarves hammering at a forge. Two more were at work crafting magnificent pieces of jewellery and swords. Their creations hung on the walls and were piled on tables. An object more beautiful than anything she had ever seen in her life caught her eye. It was a gold necklace as wide as a collar with many glittering jewels set in it. Intricate designs inspired by the forest were etched on the gold to accentuate the jewels. She desired to have it at any cost.

As she entered the hut, the dwarves stopped their work. Their eyes went wide seeing the goddess with flowing golden hair and eyes the colour of a clear summer's sky. The low sunlight behind her gave her a halo of bronze and gold. She gestured to the necklace. "I want to buy that from you. Name your price. There is no amount of gold I wouldn't pay."

They glanced at each other and the eldest of them stepped forward. "My name is Dvalin. These are my brothers, Grer, Alfrik and Berling. We are Brising dwarves. We do not require much and have all we could need. There is no price in gold you can pay. Our craftsmanship is unrivalled."

She stepped closer to him. "I will give you one minute to speak to your brothers and give me a price. Do not deny your goddess. I want the necklace."

The dwarves spoke among themselves, their voices rising and falling as they debated. Finally, the youngest one broke from the circle and approached Freyja. He wiped his forehead with a rag and smoothed out chestnut brown hair that matched his eyes. He stared at Freyja as if hypnotized.

"My fairest goddess. I am Grer. You see, this necklace is unique and incomparable, like your beauty." He lifted the necklace with a clean cotton cloth so as not sully to it with his dirty hands, and offered it to Freyja. "There is no other like this and never will be."

She took it from him and placed it on her neck. The very weight of it made it feel priceless. She didn't care how heavy it was. She wanted it even more. She imagined herself on the back of her mighty boar Hildisvíni as she gathered her share of souls on the battlefield. Freyja walked to a broad sword hanging on the wall and in its polished surface admired herself wearing the marvellous piece.

Grer spoke once more. "Therefore our price is you spend one night with each of us."

She turned around and examined the dwarves one by one. They held their breath for her response. They were all in good physical shape because of their work. Only the eldest was mildly unattractive, with less hair than the others and larger ears. Plus, she had heard that dwarves provided pleasure to women in ways that men were not creative enough to think of. And small in stature didn't mean small elsewhere. She wondered if it were true.

"I agree to your price," she said.

Grer rushed to the goddess and threw himself at her feet. He looked up at her with devotion, like a pet. "We promise to make your stay as pleasant as possible. Ask for anything and it shall be yours." He bent over and kissed the golden threads of the hem of her dress.

She continued to look at each of them, studying their excitement. "I want all of you to bathe first. Clean linens are to be provided every day and breakfast when I wake. I also expect a hot bath."

They all nodded eagerly. Grer rose to his feet. "Consider it done. Please, let me take you to our hall, where you will stay in the best room."

Freyja followed the dwarves out the hut and into the waning light.

After four days, she left with her necklace, very satisfied with her trade. It wasn't an unpleasant stay at all. She felt good.

As she walked toward the village, a shadow rushed through the trees. She looked around and, not seeing anything or anyone, continued on her way home.

Loki, the sly, shapeshifting trickster, took long, confident strides through Valhalla. He couldn't wait to tell Odin this little piece of information that would cause the type of chaos Loki thrived on and used to his advantage. Odin would owe him now.

Odin sat by his hearth and turned to see Loki approaching. He glanced up with his one good eye. "What brings you here today? I did not send for you."

Loki gave him a half-smile. "I have come across something that might interest you. Your dearest Freyja has purchased an item at a very high price." His voice could charm a butcher into buying meat.

"What do I care what she does with her gold?"

Loki had a smug look on his face. "Oh, she did not purchase it with gold. She bartered with herself. It is a necklace made by four dwarves and four nights she stayed with them as payment."

Odin looked back to the fire expressionless. Loki gave him a hard stare, surprised by his reaction. He had hoped for more. He turned to leave.

"Wait, Loki. I have a job for you."

Loki turned with a sinister gleam in his eye. "Yes, what do you ask of me?"

Odin continued to stare into the fire. "You are to retrieve this necklace without her knowledge and bring it to me."

"But no one can get into Freyja's hall!" Loki was caught off guard by this unexpectedly formidable task.

"Find a way. Remember, you came to me with this. What did you expect would happen?" Odin waved him off and Loki knew he had to leave.

He headed straight for Freyja's domain Fólkvangr, to find her impenetrable fortress.

When he arrived, Loki walked through the field, wondering how he would get inside. He was known for being clever and now he had to come up with a plan and quick. A bee buzzed past his face and continued to circle him. He swatted at it, annoyed at the distraction as he tried to think.

Then he stopped. He smirked, feeling pleased with himself, before turning himself into a fly.

Loki flew around the outside of the hall looking for a way in, but the walls seemed impenetrable. Then he reached the door, where there was a keyhole large enough to pass though. He buzzed through each room until he found Freyja. By a stroke of luck, she was asleep. But now he had the challenge of getting the necklace off her.

He gently touched her cheek with his wings. She muttered sleepily at the sensation, but didn't move. He tried her ear. This time she stirred and turned to her side. Seizing his chance, he turned back to his normal form and with his fingertips unclasped the necklace and removed it. With soft steps he walked out of the hall and back to Odin.

Freyja awoke from her sleep feeling refreshed. She touched her neck and jolted upright. She felt her neck again with both hands, then jumped out of bed. She tossed aside animal furs, pillows and blankets. She searched the floor. Her eyes narrowed. The necklace could have only been taken by magic, and she knew only one trickster who would dare. She had to see Odin.

She went straight to Valhalla, where Odin stood waiting for her by his hearth, his favourite spot in the hall. He poured two steins of mead.

"Why mead? You do not know why I am here."

He handed her a stein. "Then tell me. Your presence is celebration enough to drink."

"I had something taken from me. It is very precious and I paid a high price for it."

He lifted a leather cloth from the table. Her necklace lay beneath. Freyja took a sip of her drink. Knowing Odin, he did not offer this from the kindness of his heart.

"I see you already know ... what do you want in return for restoring it to me?"

"My price?" he said in a gruff voice that betrayed his displeasure with her. His eyes narrowed as he glared at her with anger.

She didn't appear amused or respond to his emotions. "Yes."

He looked into her eyes. "I want you to create magical enmity between two kings. Their armies will wage battle forevermore, their ranks rising again when they die. Create a war without end between them."

"That is all? And we shall never speak of this again?"

"You have my word, Freyja."

"I will agree to your price because what do I care of what men do to each other. I want my property back. But please tell Loki to stay the hell out of my hall."

Odin grunted. "Then we have a deal."

Freyja – Goddess of Fertility and Magic

Freyja translates to "a mature woman who receives respect". She is the Norse goddess of sex, fertility, magic and war.

Freyja comes from the Vanir tribe, known for their knowledge of *seiðr* or magic and fertility (fertility in all things natural, not just human fertility). Her magic was so great that Odin asked her to bestow her insights upon him. Like other Vanir, Freyja can see into the future. One of her magical items is a cloak made of falcon feathers. It allows the wearer to transform into a falcon and fly.

She is often portrayed on a chariot pulled by two cats (yes, cats!), and her familiar is a battle boar named Hildisvíni. She rides upon his back collecting her half-share of the warriors fallen in battle. Pigs are sacred to Freyja, so at Christmas they were sacrificed and eaten to honour her.

She lives in a field called Fólkvangr, in a hall named Sessrúmnir, which is magically locked. She brings her share of the dead on the battlefield to Fólkvangr, while Odin takes his share to Valhalla.

Those wanting to read about Freyja in a primary source can look up the *Poetic Edda*, a collection of medieval narrative poems compiled in Old Norse in the thirteenth century.

Freyja Wisdom

What a woman does with her body in any circumstance is her choice. It is no one else's business. This story is a reminder that someone else's opinion of a woman's choice has nothing to do with her expression of autonomy. Frejya chose to use her body and beauty as currency. Some might look down on this or weaponize their hate, but that comes from a patriarchal point of view. A woman doesn't need financial security by playing the traditional roles of wife and mother if she can provide it for herself, and she may choose to use her body as a tool to achieve this. Sex work is valid work.

The Morrigan

The Second Battle of Moytura

Samhain, the liminal and auspicious time when the long, warm days of summer are a distant memory and darkness rules the land. The worlds of the seen and unseen merge, moving closer together like an eclipse. Shadow and light become one. The living and the dead cross paths in the fields, the forests and the night. Bright fires illuminate the cold evenings now that the harvest is finally done, and the slaughtering of cattle can be heard all around. People drink and feast. That is Samhain.

During this time, the Morrigan, in her dark beauty, waited on the edge of the celebrations, near the rushing River Unshin. She bathed in the cool waters until her husband Dagda arrived to satisfy her. But it wasn't just she who wanted this. Her lovemaking, their supernatural union, could bring abundance for farmers the following spring. The rain clouds that had lingered throughout the day parted as the sun began to set. The entire sky appeared aflame in burnt orange and blood-tinged hues of red.

On this particular night, they joined to give each other pleasure and to discuss the forthcoming battle with their old foes the Fomorians. This fierce tribe of monstrous invaders from the sea and beneath the earth had to be defeated. The fight would continue until the battlefield had crushed their bones and all their ambitions. This would be the second battle of Moytura – they had defeated the Fir Bolg people in the first. The Morrigan was not unfamiliar with or afraid of war; in fact she would join the fight when the time arrived.

In the distance she could see the god Dagda, the Druid leader of the Tuatha Dé Danann, approaching her with staff in hand. He, the master of life and death, of the seasons and magic, was worthy of her on that night. Both held the secrets of death and magic.

He stood before her with his long straw-like beard streaked with pale amber and grey. His cloak hid his body and his hood shaded his eyes. But she could still feel the intensity of his gaze as he looked upon her radiant dark beauty.

"What is your council this night?" he asked, as he grazed her bare shoulder with his fingertips, then let his hand slip toward her breast. She stepped closer to him and touched his bare chest beneath his cloak. She lightly teased the bristles of hair. "You should gather all our people on the battlefield. There should be none but warriors ready to fight. I will find their king, and with magic I will drain the blood from his heart and his kidneys. The rest we shall allow fate to move, as the clouds do."

He touched her smooth skin and brushed her long, dark hair from her face. "It is good fortune you are my wife and not my enemy."

She kissed his lips. "Never do anything to make me your foe."

He dropped his staff to the ground and unclipped his cloak, allowing it to fall to his feet. Beneath the moon and beside the river, they tore into each other's bodies with lovemaking as fierce as combat and their war cries were pure ecstasy.

The day of battle arrived. The Morrigan looked to the grey sky and circling crows. If it rained, the soil would overflow with blood. And the scent of rain in the air was mixed with that of fear. She closed her eyes and could feel the heartbeats of thousands of men between her ears. So many would die or be maimed, while some would live to tell the tale of that day, perhaps in a poem, song or story that would last the ages. Fate would decide. But that was the way of war and life. She took slow, sure steps toward the enemy camp, then picked up her pace before moving to a full sprint. In an instant she transformed into a crow and flew to find the Fomorian king, Indech.

Larger than any human man, the monstrous king paced by a wood at the edge of the battlefield as he waited for word. He had only three grotesque guards with him as protection. In his arrogance, he did not suspect any sort of personal attack. Flying swiftly, Morrigan slit the throat of one of his vile entourage with the sharp point of her beak. The wide gash oozed a greenish liquid that covered the monster's body as it fell to the ground. She used her crow talons on another to pluck out its black eyes. The creature shrieked in a blind panic and ran off on its tree-trunk legs, not knowing where it rushed. For the third, she turned back into her own form to rip its head from its shoulders. The monster's oblong cranium rolled toward the oversized boots of the king, who shouted in horror at the sight of the creature's staring eyes that continued to blink until the head was drained of all its blood.

Morrigan smiled at Indech. She raised a hand to cast a binding spell upon his huge limbs.

"What is this sorcery?" croaked the king. "Your silly magic is nothing!"

"Then why are you standing here unguarded and unable to move? I foretold the means of your death and now it will be so."

With one hand she punched through his belly until she could feel one of his kidneys. With a hard yank, she ripped it out, then punched though again to snatch the other one. The king's putrid mouth full of rotting teeth made the shape of an O as he looked down in disgust. But she wasn't finished with him yet. In one hand she held both kidneys and with the other she punctured his chest. He cried out in pain when her hand gripped his heart. "And now your blood will serve to give our warriors the strength they need to finish off your forces. We will drive them toward the cliffs and their demise."

One strong tug and his heart was in her hand. Indech went slack-jawed and his eyes rolled to the back of his head. She allowed his lifeless body to fall to the ground, then detached a leather pouch from his belt and placed his organs inside. There was no time to lose: she could hear the cries for help from the Tuatha as more fell by the minute and their spirit weakened. She turned back into a crow and flew away with the pouch in her beak, rain pelting her sleek, feathered body.

She landed on a large stone in the middle of the fray, with viscera, shouts and blood all around. The field was slick with mud and gore. The Morrigan turned back into her female form and cried out to her people, as she raised the pouch containing the king's organs above her head. Her hair blew in the wind, matted with carrion. "This is what is left of their king. His life is now mine. Do not relent! It is their blood or yours this day! Finish them!" Both hands dripped with deep crimson. Her nails were like black crescent moons, caked with flesh. Streaks of dried and wet blood ran down her arms and saturated her leather bodice. Indech's blood trailed down the length of her body and over the rock. It would flow until it reached and merged with the very river where she had made love to her husband.

Hearing her encouragement, the warriors shouted in unison. They looked upon her presence, which incited terror in their enemies, with devotion and trust. She did not abandon them in their time of need. The inhuman faces of the Fomorians twisted in fury and fear as the Tuatha found another burst of rage to fight on, harder than before. No one wanted a third battle. It had to be done.

The Fomorians faced a monster greater than them. And more powerful – the Morrigan.

The battle continued with vicious bloodshed until the Fomorians retreated to the sea. The Morrigan stood before those who remained. Her people. Their bodies were broken but not their spirit. She gave them a prophecy that would bestow upon them and their families years of abundance, prosperity and peace.

The Morrigan – Mistress of War and Prophecy

Every interpretation of the name of this Celtic goddess includes *queen*. Queen of war or death, or phantom queen. Her vicious power entitles her to be regarded as such.

The Morrigan is the crow that can be seen on the battlefield or wherever there is death. She is war and carnage. She is also fate, because is not death the ultimate fate of humans?

As she comes from a tribe of supernatural beings, the Tuatha Dé Danann, she holds special powers within the realm of magic. She is also known to shapeshift. In one tale, in pursuit of a man she desires, the warrior Cú Chulainn, she turns into an eel, a cow and a wolf.

To some, she is a triple goddess, along with her two sisters Badb and Macha. Others recognize the war goddess Nemain to be associated with her. As with all tales passed down through the oral tradition, there are variants of her story from different eras and locations.

One ancient place associated with the Morrigan is a cave in County Roscommon. This is Oweynagat cave, "the cave of cats", described as the Gate to Hell. It is said to be Morrigan's home and to offer a way into the otherworld. The entrance, a small stone-lined opening surrounded by trees and grass, appears unremarkable from the outside. As you climb down, however, you find yourself in a Neolithic souterrain, a tunnel that resembles a birth canal, which then opens up to a natural cave with dagger-like stalactites. To read more about this place, begin with the twelfth-century Irish manuscript called the Book of Leinster. Mythological texts in Irish featuring the Morrigan include the Cath Maige Tuired and Táin Bó Regamma.

The Morrigan Wisdom

We all face battles in our lives. Some are short-lived while others drag on or are repeated over and over again. No matter what you may face, maintain your courage, even if the odds are not in your favour. If there happens to be no one to rally you for the fight, you can do this yourself. Self-encouragement is powerful and so is encouraging others, if you have the opportunity to do so. Words have great impact.

The Morrigan doesn't run away from a battle. Why could this be? She knows who she is and she knows the depth of her power, even in the face of a great foe. Know your power in all circumstances, especially the difficult ones.

AMATERASU

Punishment is Best Served Dark

The High Celestial Plain, the divine land where the kamis resided, is where the sun goddess Amaterasu retreated to after the confrontation with her brother, the storm god Susanoo. The tranquility of the weaving hall in her palace calmed the goddess and restored her usual bright disposition.

Acting like a spoiled child after he lost a challenge with his sister to see who could create more divine beings, Susanoo flung his shit at her palace walls and created havoc in her paddy fields and irrigation ditches. Some were destroyed completely and others were left in need of repair, which would impact the harvest in the fall. His temper could not be contained, and Amaterasu no longer had any patience for it. She would make excuses for him no longer. It was from *her* necklace that five more deities had been created. He could create only three from his sword. Her necklace was more powerful than his sword. She had won the challenge in all fairness, but he just couldn't see it that way. So Amaterasu sat peacefully in the hall with her weaving maiden. Together they worked in silence, the chirruping of birds and insects the only other sounds. Peace and quiet.

The wind whipped against a window and blew it open. The sky had turned dark and unsettled. Their hair flew into their faces with a sudden fierce gust, blocking their view of the large hole that had appeared above their heads, where the roof had been torn off.

"What is he doing now?" said Amaterasu to her maiden. She knew the storm god, her younger brother Susanoo, had to be behind this intrusion.

Her cheeks burned when she thought of his rudeness. She wished he could be banished forever.

They stared at the gaping hole. Something was approaching from the dark sky. A small dot at first, it became larger and larger. Their eyes widened with terror and disgust to see one of the celestial horses, killed and skinned, spinning toward them. The corpse fell through the hole into Amaterasu's hall. Its legs and head came away from its body and scattered in different directions as it hit the ground. Large, vacant eyes stared wide open. The weaving maiden cried out as a river of blood poured from the dead animal and covered the floor. In her fright she jumped to her feet, and as she did so her weaving shuttle stabbed her pelvis. Bright blooms of red stained her dress. Whimpers of pain escaped the maiden's lips and all colour drained from her face as the blood poured out of her. She collapsed to the ground.

Amaterasu ran to her aid, but her weaving maiden was already dead. Tears streamed from her eyes, sadness clouding her vison like the stormy sky. Her dear companion was gone.

"How dare you?" shouted Amaterasu through the hole in the roof. "How could you! I do not want to see you or anyone else ever again!"

But she knew her wicked and capricious brother didn't care. And neither would anyone else. Amaterasu rose to her feet and left her palace. She began to walk to the Heavenly Rock Cave where she would remain, taking her light and warmth with her. Something inside her had dimmed. The sun couldn't shine like this.

She climbed until she reached the open mouth of the cave and continued inside to its darkest depths. And as she retreated into the cave, so did the sun retreat from the world. A large rock rolled toward the entrance and sealed it shut.

Everything and everyone was plunged into darkness.

The kamis, the spirits of her realm, gathered to discuss what to do. Each one had a different idea. Omohikane, who was known to be very wise, was decisive. "This is what we will do. I shall find a large sakaki tree and place it next to the cave opening. On its branches I will hang a beautiful necklace, a mirror, a blue cloth and a white cloth, to draw her out."

"I shall pray," said Ame-no-Koyane-no-Mikoto.

The kamis watched to see if their prayers and offerings would be enough to lure the goddess out. They waited and waited in the dark. The cold made them shiver as they watched for any sign of her emerging.

With each hour that passed, they grew more despondent.

The goddess Ame-no-Uzume-no-Mikoto watched in silence until at last she spoke. "Look at you! What is any of this going to do? Let me try. This situation needs something more dramatic."

She adorned her hair with bamboo leaves and masaki branches. Without music she began to dance like a woman possessed. She contorted her face, then began to undress like a manic seductress. As she exposed more of her body, the other kamis began to laugh at the hysterical performance. It caused quite a ruckus.

Inside the cave, Amaterasu could hear the laughter echo. She wondered what was happening outside. Slowly she walked toward the entrance and removed the large rock that sealed the cave opening. She poked her head out. "What is going on out here?"

One of the kamis continued to laugh with tears in his eyes. "It's like nothing you've ever seen before! And just so you know, there is a goddess more beautiful than you."

Amaterasu leaned through the opening to see for herself. A kami shoved the mirror hanging from the tree in front of her. Her own reflection dazzled her – such beauty and light! It stopped her from slipping back inside. The half-naked dancing goddess saw her chance. She grabbed Amaterasu by the arm and dragged her completely out of the cave. One of the other kamis sealed the entrance so Amaterasu couldn't run back in.

Darkness gave way to the light once more as Amaterasu took her rightful place in the order of things. And Susanoo was banished from the Celestial Plane for his constant horrendous behaviour.

Amaterasu – A Brilliant Star

In the Japanese Shinto religion, Amaterasu is the sun goddess. She has two siblings: the moon god (Tsukuyomi-no-Mikoto), and the storm god (Susanoo) as described in the myth told here. She has one son from her marriage to her brother Tsukiyomi.

She is the rising sun as seen on the Japanese flag. The Imperial family is said to be of her lineage, claiming her as their direct ancestor. This story features one of the three sacred objects in the Imperial Regalia of Japan, the mirror – the other two are the sword and the jewel. Legend has it that these items were passed by Amaterasu to her grandson and then handed down through the ages.

The prominent Shinto Ise Shrine is the most famous place to worship Amaterasu. It's located at Ise in Mie Prefecture, Japan. The cave believed to feature in this myth is at the Amano Iwato Shrine at Takachiho, Miyazaki Prefecture.

Ravens are said to be Amaterasu's messengers and cocks are associated with her because they alert us to the dawn.

You can read more about Amaterasu in the *Kojiki* (Records of Ancient Matters) and the *Nihon Shoki*. Both these eighth-century texts contain the stories from Shinto mythology.

Amaterasu Wisdom

Retreating for a spell is not the same as hiding. Never feel you have to dim your own light because of feelings of shame or guilt imposed by the opinions of others or values that are not truly your own. It is perfectly okay, however, to take time for yourself to rest or to get to know your shadow self. In the tale, the goddess leaves the world to grieve, even though it means plunging everyone and everything into darkness and chaos. She needs time to grieve the pain experienced because of her problematic brother and the death of her handmaiden. There is an expectation for women to be strong and always show up, or as in the case of Amaterasu, for them to "shine". Yes, the divine feminine can be a fountain of abundance, but fountains can also run dry. You don't have to shine all the time.

SEKHMET

I Am Woman Hear Me Roar

The mighty sun god Ra watched humanity with growing fury. Their disobedience and lack of self-control made him regret their existence. Humanity had lost their sense of Ma'at, or justice and order. They could not go on like this. As he continued to observe in silence, his rage travelled from his belly to his right eye. It grew brighter and hotter until it blinded him. He could not see anything besides that flame of vitriol. He plucked the fire from his eye and held it in the palm of his giant hand. "What shall I do with you?"

The fire danced, burning orange and yellow. As it morphed into the shape of the head of a baying beast with gnashing jaws, Ra's imagination was sparked. "I shall bring you forth to show humanity the error of their ways. You shall be punishment, destruction and justice for those who deserve the sharp points of your teeth on their neck."

Ra created Sekhmet from the fire he took from his eye. And like a righteous flame, she would burn across the land. Her devouring thirst and hunger, blazing like the sun, would force the humans to appreciate their lives – and appreciate Ra too. Every heart she swallowed would be judged by Anubis on the scales against a feather representing Ma'at. Which would be heavier? Those hearts that weighed more would be consumed by Ammit – eater of the dead – and the souls denied entry to the afterlife.

When his lion-headed daughter was fully formed, he placed her at the edge of a village and allowed her to roam. She let out a roar with a blast of hot breath, intent on consuming anyone and everything in her way. Slowly she prowled toward the unsuspecting villagers.

Sekhmet pounced on village after village with her restless hunger. At first, Ra felt pleased with himself. Her retribution was swift and unmerciful. Blood saturated the sand like rain. The villagers fled, if they could, from her roars. Their tears and prayers to Ra gave him the satisfaction he desired; however, the din of those voices was beginning to fade. Something dawned on Ra: what happens after total annihilation? Who would be left to continue their worship of him?

He wanted only to rein in the humans, not get rid of them entirely. He didn't want to destroy Sekhmet his daughter, either. "Sekhmet, come back to me. You have finished."

She roared into the wind and continued on, her nose pressed to the ground, sniffing for fresh meat. Her thirst and hunger blazed. Just as the sun could not be darkened with all the water on earth, her bloodlust knew no bounds. "Sekhmet!" Ra's voice boomed, yet still she did not stop her pursuit. He had to think of a plan before she destroyed everything.

Ra made himself known to the brewers in the form of a falcon. The men were cowering in their village after learning of Sekhmet heading their way.

"I have a mission for you."

They fell to their knees, hearing a falcon speak to them. "What would you ask of us?"

"You must flood your fields and the river with all the beer you have and all that is in the surrounding villages. First dye it with red ochre until it looks like blood."

"But she is out there!" cried one of them.

"Yes, and if you want your families to survive then you will do this without question."

They bowed in reverence and agreed.

Ra flew into the clear sky, hoping his plan would be enough to stop his daughter.

The brewers did exactly as they were told, dying all their beer with red ochre and using it to stain the Nile and flood the fields. It appeared as if a great battle had taken place, with hundreds of bodies drained of their blood. Their task complete, they retreated into their homes and waited for the lioness to appear.

When Sekhmet looked upon the Nile and the fields, she licked her thick, white teeth. It was more blood than she could ever hope for. She rushed to the bank of the river and kneeled to greedily lap up the beer, still thinking it was blood. It clung to the fur on her face, dripped from her whiskers and soaked her dress. As she continued to drink, her body swayed. Her arms struggled to hold her weight and her eyes drooped with the heaviness of inebriation. Sekhmet was drunk. She fell to the ground and looked to the darkened sky before her eyes could no longer remain open. Half-roars and snores escaped her gaping mouth still wet with dyed beer. As slumber took over, the lioness and her thirst were quelled, never to be set upon humanity ever again.

Sekhmet – Destroyer and Healer

With her lioness head and female body, Sekhmet is the very definition of *I am woman hear me roar*. She is often depicted with a sun disc on her head, with a cobra (uraeus). The serpent represents her divinity. In the Egyptian religion, she was the goddess of war and controlled plagues and was the protector of pharaohs, but she was also worshipped for her ability to heal and ward off disease. She was the patron of physicians. Sekhmet's dual power is what makes her a formidable goddess.

Cats were often mummified, and some worshippers whispered their petitions to them and offered them to Sekhmet. There was a festival dedicated to the drunkenness of Sekhmet, as described in this story. In Ancient Egypt, the Tekh festival was an annual celebration of copious amounts of alcohol, music and dancing, which took place in places of worship and private homes. It wasn't uncommon for participants to drink until they passed out like Sekhmet as she drank the dyed beer. The original texts referencing Sekhmet include the tales and hymns inscribed on coffins and the very walls of the pyramids. They are respectively called the Coffin Texts and the Pyramid Texts.

Now, you may think this tale sounds familiar and you wouldn't be wrong. Scholars have noticed that it is very close to the story of Kali, who also nearly wiped out humanity. Women of wrath have a place across cultures, just like the tale of a worldwide flood.

Sekhmet Wisdom

There are times when we must observe and remain still like a cat. But there are other times when we must dig deep and use our roar. There is a difference, however, between blind rage and constructive anger. It is okay to express dissatisfaction, hurt or anger when wronged, but vitriol can be toxic if held on to for too long or if vengeance becomes a way to return cruelty. Someone may make your blood boil and you might want to rip their head off, but what does that say about you? Your experience of life should be about you, not about another person. Believe that if someone has wronged you, they will get their just desserts in due time.

Isis

Resurrection of a King

Osiris ruled over Egypt with confidence and fairness, like those who had come before him in a long bloodline of divine royalty. For Osiris, Ma'at, or justice and order, had to prevail over chaos in his kingdom. His people respected his rule and their lives reflected this. By his side was his beloved wife, Isis. Her black hair fell straight to her bronzed shoulders and her beauty was known throughout the kingdom. Although they were childless, it did not cause strife between the two. They both knew it would happen when it was meant to happen.

In the shadows of the court lurked Set. He watched Isis and Osiris with envy as they drank wine and laughed during feasts. His ears wanted to bleed when others lavished praise on Osiris. On these occasions, Set's smile had to hide the deep hatred that made him feel sick when he heard his brother speak of his deeds and the prosperity of the kingdom. *It should be me on that throne,* he would tell himself. *I could create ten times the wealth he has. My name would be known far beyond the borders of this kingdom.* Always the forgotten brother, he began to shape his lethal plan.

Quietly, he had gathered friends, those who held secret grudges against Osiris. He wouldn't be unknown for long. He had to act fast before an heir was produced – that would complicate the matter. Another feast was scheduled very soon and Set had a special surprise for the adored ruler Osiris. And even better, it would break Isis. He couldn't wait to see her tears and hear her wails.

Osiris wandered with Isis back to their chambers after the feast. Set emerged from a dark corner of the gardens. "My dear brother, we did not get to speak at all this night. Can you spare a moment now?"

"Tonight was a very busy evening," Osiris agreed. He looked to Isis, not suspicious about his brother's request. "I will join you later."

Isis studied Set's face. She didn't trust him. He always managed to find himself entangled in strife or violence. His demeanour was the exact opposite of Osiris's. And she knew he was devious. Not once had he ever requested a private audience in this manner. He was up to something. She could feel it in her bones. A gnawing sense of dread made the hairs on her body stand upright. But she couldn't pinpoint exactly what was causing her unease, and lingering would not make him reveal it.

"I will see you later, my husband."

Set gave her a nod and walked into a darkened path with Osiris. Isis rushed to her chamber and caught their loyal servant, who stood by every night.

"I want you to run to the gardens and follow Set and Osiris. Do not make yourself known under any circumstances. Then report back to me."

The servant did as he was told. Isis would not sleep until she had heard from him or Osiris had returned to inform her what Set wanted.

The gardens were empty at that time of night. "Now, what do you want, brother? We have walked for some time and you have not said anything."

Set stopped beside a solitary lit torch. "Because I have nothing to say. It is what I am about to do that matters."

A large soldier with arms as thick as a man's head jumped from the brush. With a single swipe, he decapitated Osiris. The spinal column made a loud crack as it broke. Head and body fell to the ground with a hard thud. The soldier took a step closer to the body, but Set snatched the blade from his co-conspirator. "Give that to me. I want the pleasure of ensuring he is lost forever and never loved by anyone again."

Set's eyes were ablaze with murderous rapture as he looked at Osiris's limp body. The blade had been sharpened specifically for this reason and the flesh would sever easily. He raised his arms and chopped off each of Osiris's limbs at the joint, then cut through other joints until there were too many pieces for anyone to want to recover. He lifted the king's head by the hair and looked into the open eyes. "Who is clever now, brother? You never saw this coming. You made this too easy for me, soft ruler that you were. Now the kingdom will see what a real king is like."

Set's soldiers held their noses against the stench as the body released its fluids, but not Set. He breathed in death like it was a perfume. He turned to them. "I want his corpse scattered far and wide. There are no kingdoms for rotting, strewn pieces of flesh. He will never be a man again."

They nodded and proceeded to obey his orders.

Isis paced until the door swung open. She hoped it would be Osiris. Instead, it was the servant with red eyes and tear-sodden face. He fell to his knees. "The king! He is dead! Set had him murdered! His body will be flung to every corner of the kingdom, never to be found again."

Isis could not comprehend the words she heard. This couldn't be correct. "Get my sister. Now!"

The servant leapt to his feet. Not minutes later Nephyths rushed into the chamber. Isis stood by an open window overlooking the Nile. She held onto the wall for support as tears streamed down her cheeks.

Crying too, Nephyths embraced her sister. "I cannot believe what I have been told. What will you do?"

"There is only one way and that is through the power of the unseen, through magic ... I must find the scattered parts of his body first."

Nephyths nodded her head. "Yes, you must. If I can be of any assistance, I will be. But what can you do even if all of him is recovered?"

Isis wiped her tears. Her expression hardened. "Bring him back and take the throne from Set. Otherwise all the work Osiris has accomplished in establishing the rule of justice will be undone."

"You must know that Set will remind everyone that you have no heir. He wants those who loved Osiris and you to turn from any hope. He wants the memory of Osiris to be erased from history. Why else scatter his body like that?"

Isis shook her head. "Ma'at must be restored." She closed her eyes. "I will find every last piece of him, but I must leave now before Set decides to rid the court of me too."

She transformed into a falcon and fled into the moonlight to find the body of the rightful king and bring him back to life.

Isis flew far and wide, using her instincts to find all the pieces of Osiris as they were dispersed over the next few weeks. She kept herself hidden so as not to alert Set to her plan. Bit by bit she gathered her beloved Osiris and carried him to an abandoned hut at the edge of the Nile. It had once belonged to a ferryman, before the dock was moved to its new location, and she often used it as a place to escape the royal court when she needed peace and quiet. There was no one around to see what she was doing.

Isis transformed to her human form and gathered the pieces of Osiris's body on a table, arranging them in a crude semblance of his form. She lit candles and tied ropes with magical knots to surround the body. She closed her eyes. "Thoth, I call on you to come to me and share with me your divine wisdom. Anubis, lord of preserving the flesh. Come to me and grant me your knowledge."

There was no light from the moon or stars that night. Isis had only the candle flames to help her see in the darkness. They burned like her desire to see justice served. A wind blew through the open window, snuffing out the candles. She could hear heavy breathing, then glowing yellow eyes and white fangs appeared.

The flames ignited again, brighter than before. It was Anubis, the jackal-headed god.

Isis looked into his eyes. "You heard me."

"Yes," he growled.

"And I," whispered a raspy voice as soft as the wind. "A great injustice has occurred here."

"Osiris and I have no heir and Set sits on the throne as the kingdom grows more out of control by the day. There is violence and a shortage of grain. Help me to restore Osiris and the rule of order and justice before it is too late."

Anubis extended his hands toward Isis. He held linen and resin. "The body must be complete."

Thoth also held out his hands. "Here are amulets to amplify the magic as we recreate his body."

"And after?"

"He will rise once more and there will be hope for an heir."

Tears welled in her eyes. "Thank you."

She took the cloth from Anubis and they began to prepare the body. Isis worked tirelessly, whispering spells and taking care to ensure the body would be intact. By sunrise, Osiris was a complete man again.

"He needs air to fill him again," said Thoth. "Breath is the last component needed for this to work."

Isis brought her mouth to Osiris's and strove without success to push her own breath into his body. She thought of her journey to find him, the way she soared through the air in the form of a falcon. She turned into a bird again and flapped her wings in rhythmic movements over the entire length of his body and over his face. The air disturbed the whole hut, knocking over candles, chairs, tableware on the shelves. She poured all her energy into creating a vortex above her husband to bring him back to life and to create life within herself.

With a loud gasp from his mouth, Osiris's eyes snapped open. Isis continued to fly up and down his body, flapping her wings and stroking him with her feathers, until he sat upright. She landed on a chair next to the table, then became human again.

She embraced him and he slowly wrapped his arms around her. "I cannot believe I am here with you again."

Thoth touched her shoulder. "Isis, you will no longer be alone."

She looked toward her belly and placed both hands over her womb.

Osiris touched her cheek. "My dear queen, I would not be resurrected without you. I owe you everything."

"I and our child will see that you are avenged. No matter how long it takes, Set will be removed from the throne."

"If anyone can make this right then it is you, Isis, most powerful of them all. No god has ever brought a loved one back from the dead."

Anubis stepped forward. "The time has come, Osiris. You have work to do elsewhere."

Osiris nodded, understanding in his eyes. "I must take my place as a ruler of another kingdom, the domain of the dead."

Isis and Osiris embraced. She smiled and said, "Until we meet again, dear one."

Isis – Queen of Passion

The first written mentions of Isis were found in the Pyramid texts, which are stories carved into the walls of Ancient Egyptian burial chambers. The tale I have told here is one variant of the Osiris and Isis myth. The other version comes from the first-century Greek philosopher Plutarch, who filled in gaps left in the original Egyptian text and gave a different account of Osiris's death, in which he was tricked to climb into a chest that was then sealed and thrown into the Nile.

Isis is the name the Greeks eventually called her; the original Egyptian form of her name was Aset. Her names mean throne. She is connected to death, divine healing, resurrection and motherhood. She is a protector of women. She is mother to Horus, who is sometimes seen in statues at her breast. Horus is a sky god who appears as a falcon.

Upon her head she wears the sun disc between two horns, with a cobra (uraeus – a staple for Egyptian deities) that signifies her divinity. What Isis is most known for, her superpower, is her magic. One of her most iconic images shows her in a kneeling position, arms outstretched with a full set of falcon wings.

An important symbol for this goddess is the tyet, the Isis knot, which is associated with her blood. In Egyptian magic, the knot is used in spell work to bind and release. Examples of the Isis knot survive as amulets created from various stones and metals, which were left with entombed bodies for protection in the afterlife. Blood-red stone was preferred, as instructed in the Egyptian Book of the Dead. The Isis knot is also known as the tit (pronounced teet), and the loop part of the knot does indeed look like a breast capped with a nipple.

Isis's temples began in Egypt and later cropped up in various locations as her stories travelled through the Roman Empire. Her powers and attributes expanded as devotion to her spread over time and distance, until she became the important deity we know today.

Isis Wisdom

Rebirth is possible in any period of your life. It is never too late to reinvent yourself and discover your inner magic. Isis knew she wasn't just the wife of a powerful king. She took it upon herself to find a seemingly impossible solution to her grief. She wanted to defy death. And she did.

Inner magic can be used by anyone. You may not be able to transform into a bird, but your mind can defy the limits of what others believe possible. Don't discount your inner magic.

Spider Grandmother

The Web of Life

Spider Grandmother awoke in an instant and sat bolt upright. White threads of hair fell over her brow. She brought her hand to her face and touched her skin. The softness and deep grooves felt familiar, even if she did not know what any of this was. She looked at her brown hands. Some of her fingers were crooked. The skin sank on her bones so she could see the thick veins like the legs of a spider. With the softness of a feather, wisdom, deep knowing, compassion and creativity floated within her spirit.

She looked around and saw another with skin a deeper hue of brown than hers and very tall. He kneeled next to her. "I am Sotuknang. Tawa, the great god of the sun, gave me instruction to create. And so here you are. I would like you to do the same." He pointed to the sky, where the blazing sun shone upon them. She had to cover her eyes from the brightness.

Deep within her, she knew what she had to do. Her purpose had been seeded as instinct. Her long, thin fingers touched the clay beneath her. It felt dry and hard. Not very good for her task. With this earth she would create something divine. She moved her lips and mouth to create more saliva. This water pooling in her mouth would soften the hard earth to make it malleable.

With patience and grace, she used her saliva and the clay to create two beings like Sotuknang. But these creations remained still and silent. There was a void within them. With her hands and thoughts, she imagined weaving a large, white blanket. This would be the fabric of consciousness, the ability to be aware in the same way she was. She covered her two creations with the blanket. Her lips moved and her voice emerged to sing a song that would breathe life over them.

From beneath the cloth, she could see movement, so she removed the covering. Two beings blinked at her. She smiled. "You are Poqanghoya and you are Palongawhoya. Each of you shall go to the opposite ends of the earth and keep it balanced."

She then went to work creating all the plant life that would make the world beautiful and unique: trees, bushes, flowers. In her giant web of life, this great dream she weaved, her creations all had different qualities to be used for the benefit of themselves and others. It all worked in complete harmony, like a song.

Her mind switched to the creatures. She created all types of animals, birds and insects, all made from her saliva, the soil and the white fabric of consciousness. Finally, with the same mixture of things, she made four beings like the first male humans, and four like her, the opposite. Once complete, she covered them with the fabric of consciousness. Yet, when they awoke, they could not speak.

"Sotuknang," she called out. "They need speech and the knowledge of how to create more of themselves, so the earth might be full and joyful."

"I shall do this."

Sotuknang looked at the humans with their eyes wide, foreheads glistening with sweat, and the circular soft spot on the crown of their heads pulsing at the same pace as their hearts.

"Listen to me. You must always remember your Creator and have respect for him. Live in harmony with one another and with this beautiful place you inhabit."

"There, just over the horizon, is your father. Remember," he said to them.

The beings looked to the sun. Heat and bright rays dried their sweat and hardened the spot on their heads.

"This world is called Topkela," said Spider Grandmother.

For a while it was bliss, but as time passed, discord, domination and rivalry began to create the chaos of war. They neither respected nor remembered the Creator.

Sotuknang did not like this. A chosen few who had remained faithful to the Creator followed a cloud to the kiva of the Ant People, to live underground while the First World was destroyed. When they arrived, Sotuknang appeared and spoke to them once more. "Learn from the Ant People while you are here. They can show you skills and a way of life that honours the Creator."

Sotuknang left the few and incinerated the world to smouldering ruins, then rebuilt it to create the Second World, Topka. Again, the humans began by living in harmony with nature, but as they created villages and commerce, their greed overcame their remembrance of the Creator. Once more, a select few went underground with the Ant People while Sotuknang destroyed the earth with a great freeze. No one above ground survived.

When the ice thawed and the sun warmed the land again, the chosen humans were allowed out to the Third World, Kuskurza. Sotuknang looked at them sternly. "You must go forth and respect, praise and honour me and the Creator. Live in harmony. If you do not, there will be consequences."

The pattern began once more. The number of humans increased and so did their penchant for ever greater wars with more powerful weapons. The slaughter did not go unnoticed. This time Sotuknang called upon Spider Grandmother. "Please do what you can to save the few who remain faithful. The world will be destroyed by a great flood."

Spider Grandmother's thoughts turned to all her creations. She used hollow reeds, which were waterproof and would float, to save the chosen from drowning. Inside she left water and cornmeal so they would not starve. She gave them a soft smile. "I will not forget you. When the time is right, I will be back. Wait for me." Then she closed the ends until the storm was over and the waters receded.

The reeds rocked and moved with the waves until they landed on the ridge of a mountain. Spider Grandmother saw that the chosen were stuck and still surrounded by nothing but water. She opened the reeds for the humans to step onto solid ground once more.

Spider Grandmother gazed out to the horizon. "You must now continue on, but I will be with you on this journey. First, you must make boats from the reeds, then we will go toward the horizon. We travel east."

The faithful listened to her and got to work without complaint or questioning, even with the hot sun blazing overhead. Once the boats were complete, they set off for another unknown destination. They rode wave after wave until they reached some islets.

"Land over there!" one of the humans called out.

Spider Grandmother narrowed her eyes that were still sharp as ever. "No. If you need to stop for a rest then we can do that, but otherwise we keep going. I will know when we have arrived."

So they continued on in the boats over the vast waters that covered the earth until a large and expansive land mass could be seen. Spider Grandmother smiled and looked to the sun.

"You may stop here. We have arrived."

Sotuknang appeared on the shore. "You have made it. This is The Fourth World, Tuwaqachi. But do not be mistaken, this world will also be destroyed if you choose not to live in harmony, and you again lose your way. The choice is yours."

Spider Grandmother – Ancient Protector

Her role is that of a mother and nurturer. As a creator goddess, Spider Grandmother brings us into being and also guides, teaches and passes on wisdom. She is benevolent. Her home is underground when she is in the form of a spider, but she does not remain there hidden, and it is not the underworld of other goddesses.

There is also another story that isn't as loving. She is said to seek out naughty children. When she closes in on them, she wraps them in a web to eat.

Spider Grandmother is a fierce champion for her people and a place to seek hope in the face of the horrors of colonization and genocide. She isn't just significant to the Hopi; the Navajo, Ojibwe, Zuni and Pueblo peoples also tell stories about her. For the Navajo, her abode is Spider Rock in Canyon de Chelly, and she is responsible for teaching them the art of weaving. This skill was not only useful for everyday life, but also represents the gift of beauty and art.

Spider Woman's Granddaughters, edited by Paula Gunn Allen, is an anthology of essays and traditional stories by Native American women which build upon creation mythology.

In pre-Colombian Mexico, the Great Goddess of Teotihuacán was also a spider goddess, but unlike Spider Grandmother, she was associated with the underworld and darkness. We don't know much about her except from her murals in Teotihuacán.

Spider Grandmother Wisdom

Life is fragile. The cycle of destruction and rebirth is a theme we see across cultures in stories of the dark feminine. In this tale, the world was destroyed multiple times. It was a powerful matriarch who offered humans protection and guided them to a new path. As we age, our wisdom and knowledge deepen, and so can our empathy and compassion. By passing our insights on to younger generations and any who come to us for guidance, we can help to create a new world. And as technology connects humans ever more closely, so we have more opportunities to deepen our understanding of each other.

Tonantzin / La Virgen de Guadalupe

Hill of Tepeyac, Mexico, 12 December 1531

Juan Diego, a Nahua man, climbed the steep hill to pray in a place that was once dedicated to his people's own goddess, who they called Tonantzin. He wasn't usually the praying type, but for some reason he felt the need to be in solitude. He wanted to sit above the village and ponder his life, as people do from time to time. It was a pleasant day with some cloud cover to shield him from the scorching rays of the sun as he climbed.

"Juan, my son," a soft voice whispered in Nahuatl, his native language. He looked around, but he didn't see anyone. The few trees and bushes were too far away for the owner of the voice to be hiding behind them.

He continued to climb until he almost reached the top.

"Juan Diego, I am here."

He turned again. This time he saw a woman standing before him, who surely had come from thin air. He knew he'd been the only person on that path as he climbed. The woman had an ethereal and mystical appearance. She was much too dark to be Spanish and her flawless bronze skin glowed. Her head and body were draped in green and white robes, and her bare feet didn't have a speck of dust on them. A sense of peace and protection cloaked him in that moment. He stared at her, mesmerized yet unsure if he could believe his eyes and ears. "Who are you and how do you know my name?" he asked.

Her energy was all-encompassing. Her voice could soothe wild beasts or a crying babe. "When you speak of me to them, you must call me Mary.

Because I look after all my people, I have come to you for a very special reason. I need you to tell others at the church to build a shrine dedicated to me in this place."

He looked confused. "Mary? The mother of Christ?" he asked. She didn't look like any of the statues or paintings the priests had brought with them. She looked like *him*. How Tonantzin the great earth mother might appear. But they'd been told not to worship her. In any case, the great earth mother did not wear robes but a skirt of snakes and a necklace made from the hands and hearts of men. She was the mother they'd had to bury and forget ever existed.

"Just call me Mary. And I need you to deliver my message."

He shook off these thoughts of the great mother. "But I'm a nobody. Why me?"

"Why not you? We are all children who come from God. Now go to Bishop Zumárraga. Tell him you saw me here."

He rushed down the hill to find the bishop, his mind racing as he tried to figure out how to approach him. The villagers were dumbfounded as Juan sped past. When he reached the gate of the mission, Spanish friars stopped him. They looked at his worn clothes and his rough hands and dark skin. "What do you want? Why do you come here out of breath and sweating?"

He swallowed hard and removed his straw hat. "I have a message for the bishop. A miracle has occurred. I have ..."

Before he could say more, two of them blocked his way. "You cannot beg for anything here. Go away." There was no kindness or mercy in their hard faces.

Feeling dejected, Juan left and went back to the hill. He had only just accepted this new faith Christianity. He had learned that his familiar gods, the gods of his ancestors, were from some demon called Satan. It only made half-sense to him. He sat alone until the voice came to him once more.

"Where are the people from the church?"

He shook his head and looked up at the beautiful, calm woman, who had to be some goddess. Maybe a new goddess who had come to help the people like him as well as the Spanish. They could share her. "The friars wanted nothing to do with me. I did ask you *why me?*"

"Go back once more. Insist, my son."

He rose to his feet and did as instructed. This time he didn't run through the village. When he approached the mission, he thought he might be in luck after all as the bishop was outside, giving a blessing to the villagers. Juan pushed through the crowd, trying to get his attention. "Bishop Zumárraga! I have an important message from the holy mother called Mary. She says we must build her a place of devotion on the hill."

One of the friars leaned close to the bishop's ear. "He may have come to Christ, but what if it is just for show? He wants to make fools of us and build another temple to their pagan goddess!"

The bishop looked at Juan Diego with suspicion. "What do you want to tell me?"

"I have seen a miracle! The one who is called Mary wants you to build a shrine to her on the hill. It is true, I promise you. Please listen to me." Juan Diego did not hold back his pleas.

There was some pity in the bishop's disbelieving stare. "Alright, if this is in fact a divine message then prove it by sending ... hmm, what shall we say .... by sending red roses!"

Juan nodded his head dolefully. Only cacti, agaves and a few trees grew on the hill where Mary appeared. He walked away feeling even more dismayed and lost than before. No one believed him. And roses?

He climbed back up the hill. The woman was there again. "Why such sorrow in your heart?"

"Because the bishop wants proof. He wants roses."

"And you doubt?"

He looked into her eyes that glowed like the sun. "I don't know what to believe. Are you our goddess Tonantzin ... or Mary ... or nothing at all?"

"Come closer."

As he did so, his nose was filled with a divine scent he had never experienced before. It was fresh, sweet and intense.

"Take off your tilma, then open your arms to me," she said.

He removed his cape and handed it to her. She brought it close to her breasts, then placed it in his arms. The sweet aroma overwhelmed him as he looked upon a miracle: the tilma was full of red roses. He held his cape gently to protect this precious gift that filled his nose with the beautiful aroma of the deep love and devotion of a mother. Of the great mother beneath his feet and in the sky, who provided humans what they needed to survive. In his heart he knew who Mary was, and no one could erase her from history.

He carried his tilma filled with roses to the bishop. As he approached, the friars stared at him speechless and allowed him to enter the mission. When he stood before Bishop Zumárraga, another miracle happened. The bishop fell to his knees, seeing the image left on the cloth of one who could only be the holy mother of Christ beneath the red roses. Juan Diego also kneeled and placed the tilma on the ground.

"We will begin work and tell the world of this miracle," said the bishop to Juan Diego. "Your name will be known beyond your life in a story people will never forget."

Tonantzin / La Virgen de Guadalupe – The Divine Feminine

In Nahuatl this tale is called Nican Mopohua or "Here It Is Told". It's about the Catholic saint La Virgen de Guadalupe (the Virgin Mary), but I wanted to show how the Indigenous beliefs were intertwined with the Catholic faith after the conquest of Mexico. La Virgen de Guadalupe's feast day is still celebrated on 12 December. The place where La Virgen showed herself to Juan Diego had long been a site where Tonantzin was worshipped. Scholars still debate whether she was an earth goddess or an aspect of the divine feminine in all Aztec goddesses. She is also known as Coatlicue.

As mentioned in the story, Tonantzin wears a skirt made from snakes and a necklace made from a skull, hearts and hands. Her statue in the Museo Nacional de Antropología in Mexico City shows her with large breasts and two snakes sprouting from her neck. The earth goddess was celebrated in the spring with a human sacrifice. It is no wonder the colonizers wanted to create a more "motherly" representation of what a goddess should be like.

The Basilica of Our Lady of Guadalupe on the Hill of Tepeyac, Mexico City, stands on the site of a temple dedicated to Tonantzin. However, it met the same fate as the Templo Mayor, the destroyed main temple of Tenochtitlan (the original name of Mexico City). Inside the basilica, you can see Juan Diego's tilma imprinted with the face of Mary, just as the Shroud of Turin is said to display the image of Jesus. In 1999, Pope John Paul II declared La Virgen de Guadalupe the patron of the Americas.

So who was the goddess exactly? Very similar to La Virgen actually. For the Indigenous population, Tonantzin was a mother goddess associated with fertility and the natural world, and so was hugely important in their culture and daily life. To this day, some still refer to La Virgen de Guadalupe as Tonantzin.

Tonantzin / La Virgen de Guadalupe Wisdom

Your identity, your essence, is a kaleidoscope of many things. Embrace this, for there is no other on this planet with the exact same measure of what makes you unique. In your true identity, you can find your soul purpose or purposes.

Some dark goddesses present themselves to us in various ways. Tonantzin meant different things to different people, and her manifestation in the world evolved. A mother goddess still known today, she bestows upon worshippers what they might need in their lives at that moment. Be open to your own gifts changing and developing once you discover them, and know that whatever you create will find the right recipients at the right time.

Baba Yaga

The Old Tales are True

"Why must I stay home and watch Sergei?"

Olga pouted as she watched her mother and father prepare to go to the market to sell firewood and bread.

"Because we will be very busy and we cannot entertain you. It will be crowded today. When he is a little older, you both can come and help."

Olga rolled her eyes. "Fine."

Her mother stopped at the door as she tied a scarf over her head, securing it beneath her chin. "Remember, if you see black geese, go inside. They are a sign that the witch Baba Yaga is near. Those creatures are unpredictable and hostile. She is even worse."

Olga wanted to roll her eyes again at this stupid tale meant for babies. She was almost fourteen.

"If you say so," she muttered.

Sergei, five years old, gave his mother and father a hug before they left. When they shut the door, Olga turned to her brother. "This is going to be a very long day. Let's go outside while the weather's still nice."

The young boy nodded and gave her a warm smile.

The sky was cloudless and the sun felt good with autumn already settling in. Sergei played with his wooden soldiers in the dirt, oblivious to Olga's look of displeasure.

A shadow crossed the ground and Olga looked up. It was just a flock of geese. She remembered what her mother had said. Part of her thought she should grab her brother and go inside; the other part of her wanted to gloat to her parents that they saw a flock of geese and nothing happened. Those tales were lies for children.

Olga was watching Sergei play, feeling bored, when, in a sudden rush, a powerful wind blew past them. The loud squawking of geese and flapping of wings filled the air. One of the geese plucked Sergei by the collar of his shirt and lifted him off the ground with its large black beak. Its eyes were bright yellow, like the flame of a candle. Olga jumped to her feet and tried to grab her brother's ankles, but another goose snapped at her. As they began to fly away, she ran beneath them, following their path. They had to have a nest somewhere. Panic made her body tremble as her legs wobbled and tears fell from her eyes.

She passed the river and saw a fish flopping on a rock. "Help! Throw me in!" it cried in a tiny voice.

It pained her to see this helpless creature suffer, so with one eye still on the geese she managed to pick up the slippery fish and toss it into the water. It made a splash and immediately a shell popped out from the water and onto the bank. The fish poked its head out. "A shell, if you should ever need help. Just throw it in the air."

She nodded and grabbed the shell before running after the geese again. Sergei's screams echoed in the forest, which had become denser and darker. As she ran through the trees, Olga heard another little voice. "Help! I don't want to get eaten."

It was a squirrel caught in a hunter's trap. She kneeled down and released it.

"Thank you. Take this acorn. Should you need help, just toss it in the air."

She took the acorn in the same fist as the shell, and continued running toward her brother's cries.

As she ran on, the leaves and branches crunching underfoot, a despairing squeak came from a hole in the ground. She stopped and looked inside. A mouse was scuttling at the bottom. "Help! I can't get out!"

She lowered her hand into the hole and opened her palm to the mouse. It crawled on and let her lift it out and place it on the ground. "Here is a stone," it squeaked. "Throw it in the air if you should need help."

She took the stone in the same fist as the shell and the acorn, and continued to follow her brother's voice. It wasn't long until she stopped at a fence made from human spinal columns and leg bones attached to each other with rusty wire. It was topped by a row of skulls peering back at her. Some had flickering candles inside. She swallowed hard and held one hand over her nose against the stench of blood and faeces. Behind the fence a house stood on large chicken legs. Each vicious claw had to be as long as her father was tall. Each one was caked with muck.

Fear and panic rooted her to the spot. She hadn't believed that this house, and even worse that Baba Yaga, really existed. She'd never ventured this far into the woods.

But she had to be brave and get her brother back. Olga walked through the gate of bones and approached the house. There was no sign of the geese. All was silent. Then she heard a soft whimpering, which seemed to be coming from a chicken coop. Inside she could see her brother. The little boy shook with terror. His face was red and smeared with snot and tears. Goose dung clung to his hair and clothing.

"Let's get out of here before Baba Yaga and her geese get back."

Sergei took her hand and climbed out of the coop. As they began to run away from the witch's horrifying home, the geese fluttered out of the dark treetops where they had been hiding. Their louds squawks were matched by the shrieks coming from Baba Yaga herself, as she left her house and took off in her flying mortar, steering with her pestle as she chased after them. Her long, hairy nose twitched. Her eyes glowed with rage. She grinned evilly, showing her yellowed teeth sharpened to points as dangerously lethal as the claws on the chicken feet. "Now I will eat up both of you! Your bones will be ground for my geese to eat."

Olga grabbed Sergei's hand as they ran through the trees. In her other hand, she squeezed the small objects she'd been given by the animals she'd helped. She tossed the shell into the air and let it fall behind her. From the opening of the shell, a lake formed. Olga's eyes widened and her heart jumped for joy as Baba Yaga was kept at bay on the far side. She seemed to be unable to fly across the magic water.

But they were not yet safe. The old witch unhinged her jaw with a sneer and a mean look in her eye and swallowed the water until her belly looked like it would burst. Then she set off in pursuit again. Her stringy hair flew behind her as she gained speed.

Next, Olga threw the acorn behind her. As soon as it hit the ground, an impenetrable barrier of trees formed. The trunks were so wide, tall and strong it seemed like they would stop even Baba Yaga. Olga exhaled deeply as the river near her family's house came into view. They were almost home.

But Baba Yaga thrashed through the trees with her teeth and the pestle. She chewed through the branches like a starving wolf. Leaves and splinters sprayed in all directions. The forest birds and animals dashed out of her way as she snarled. And then the trees were no more.

Olga had one item left, the stone. She squeezed her brother's hand before tossing it back. The stone rolled across the ground and created a mountainous rock wall that reached so high even Baba Yaga could not pass.

The witch shrieked behind the jagged wall. Olga kept hold of Sergei until they reached their home. She threw open the door and locked it shut once they were inside. She rushed to the window, but couldn't see Baba Yaga. The geese, however, were flying away. She hoped the old witch was doing the same.

Olga collapsed in relief onto her chair, never to doubt the tales of old again.

Baba Yaga – Child Eater

She is well known as a witch, but she has also been celebrated as a seasonal nature goddess of Slavic mythology. Her domain is the forest, where she lives as a recluse in a house that stands on two (sometimes four) chicken legs and is surrounded by a fence made from bones and skulls. She can will the house to move. She also rides in a mortar and uses a pestle like an oar to push herself along (how very witchy). She carries a broom to ensure her tracks are wiped away behind her.

Her stories range from hateful to helpful. They say she is a stealer of children so she can eat them, but she also helps a young woman who has escaped a Cinderella-type life with an evil stepmother. Written stories about Baba Yaga date to the nineteenth century, but as with other folk characters she has been around much longer than that. The beauty of oral storytelling is that you don't have to conform to any one version of a tale and can allow your imagination to go wild. Her folk tales include Vasilisa the Beautiful, Baba Yaga's Black Geese and The Frog Princess.

Baba Yaga Wisdom

Stories are meant to be shared. Storytelling is fun and connects us with one another. Baba Yaga's adventures, like other frightening tales, have been told for centuries. As time goes on, the storyteller might add a detail here or there or change something to adapt to a specific audience. As stories grow they become part of the collective consciousness. Keeping stories alive, especially the scary ones, feeds our imagination and makes us hungry for more. The old tales inspire new ones that will reflect the creator and the world in which they live. Telling stories is vital to humanity. Don't be afraid to share yours.

Hecate

To Die in Her Arms

A living witch can be a powerful force, but a dead one is unstoppable. That is what the elders always said. It was time we saw it happen.

I ran through the wood on the Landslip near our village, Bonchurch, with my arms pumping hard. The cold drizzle kept my senses alert. If the Patrol caught me then it would mean taking my own life. The three silver moon pendants hanging from a leather cord slapped against my sternum. Dogs barked in the distance. They were hunting me down like a fox. And like a fox I had to find some place to hide. Funny how hunting animals had been banned for years, but humans were fair game now. Everything was, now that governments had pretty much ceased to exist.

The Patrol had landed that afternoon. The Isle of Wight had seemed the safest place for our coven when the bombing started and somehow we'd managed to make our way across. The island wasn't far from the mainland, but far enough without fuel. We'd been warmly welcomed by our sisters already living there, and the coven had stayed in control of Yarmouth port for several years. But now the Patrol had come.

"Hecate, I pray, help me to find a way. Guide my steps in this life or the next," I whispered as I ran through the trees in the darkness.

The shouts of the men pursuing me were getting louder. I was thankful for the long sleeves that protected my arms as I pushed through branches and brambles. Those sleeves also hid the skeleton key tattoo on both my forearms. It the secret sign of our coven, dedicated to the goddess Hecate.

Few people knew that the Isle of Wight had been our coven's main home for centuries. No one really thinks magic exists. Not unless you practise it. Not unless you find yourself channelling the goddess herself before her altar and image. Now, society as we knew it had ended, devolving to the feral beginnings of the first humans without electricity, shopping malls or schools. Witchcraft had become a beacon for those needing guidance, and Hecate the bright flame of wisdom and strength for those who felt drawn to her. She spoke to us in dreams and visions.

I needed her help now ... and fast. The dogs were getting closer and there was no way I could make it to Bonchurch. Further down the Landslip were cliffs that fell straight into the rocks and choppy water.

The Patrol hunted witches for sex, organs and knowledge of nature. That is why we'd left the mainland. Women, and especially witches, had become a commodity. But we thrived on the Isle of Wight, and they hated us for it.

"You can't get away, love." A man in black camouflage emerged from beneath fallen trees. He held a blade in one hand. My heart raced and vison tunnelled. I was so close. I had to get back to Bonchurch. Everything inside me felt crushed. He took a walkie talkie from his belt. "You can stop the search. I found her. Go get the others."

I remained silent and touched my pendant to call on her. I had to have faith that her shadow fell upon me.

The man's dark eyes glittered with hate and lust. He licked his lips. "You witches are all the same. Deluded. There is no magic in the world. You have no real power. Submit to this fact and make your lives easier."

"We kept you off this island for this long and now we'll kill you all," I said defiantly and I meant every word. "This place is ours."

He walked closer to me with his blade in hand. "I don't think so. But I do need a new house pet. You will do fine." He smiled. Sweat glistened all over his face. This was the only chance I would have.

I snatched the blade attached to the inside of my left boot. It had been blessed by Hecate herself at the last full moon bonfire and now this asshole would be a meal for her hounds.

He rushed toward me ready to strike. I darted out of his way, making him work hard to catch me. My small, lithe body could navigate the rocky terrain better than he, and I knew this wood well. We danced around each other, each of us poised to strike. With all my strength I charged toward him with my blade raised. I slashed his face and torso. He cried out from pain and so did I as his blade pierced my belly. But I had no time to focus on that. He wasn't going to get out of this wood. The sound of crashing waves rose from the shore. It was a fine place to die, even for a cretin like him. I charged again and drove my blade into his chest before running hard past him and up the steep slope.

"Not that way," I heard in the soft breeze. I veered away, toward another path. My belly was throbbing with pain, but I ignored it. Unlike our so-called government, Hecate would not abandon me.

Every step back to the church in Bonchurch was agony, but there was no sign of the Patrol. "We need a miracle," I wept in the candle-lit darkness as I stared at the mural of Hecate. The medieval church had been converted to the worship of our goddess, and her image now covered the whole of one wall. We'd taken out the cross with its pasty body hanging in misery, unable to do anything but watch humans suffer century after century without doing a goddamn thing. Hecate, in contrast, was alive and well and looking down on me now, with her three bodies and faces and her outstretched arms. Wax from the candles had spilled over the stone floor, next to the wildflowers we picked to offer to her. Glass bowls were filled with the shells and stones we had gathered for her. Hecate showed us there could still be beauty and joy in catastrophe and times of worry. She reminded us that we had each other.

I didn't check my wound because deep down I already knew what this excruciating pain meant. In the distance I could hear dogs and the shouting of their handlers. I looked back to the mural. "Hecate, we need you now." The candles flickered and some blew out.

I had to alert the others that the Patrol were coming. Bonchurch was my station. I stumbled outside the church to the beacon we'd built to use as a signal in the event of an emergency. I lit it and let it blaze. There were always witches on watch for smoke and fire in the sky. It was all we had now to communicate across the island.

The men and dogs were among the gravestones of the churchyard now and I resigned myself to death. But as I tried to stumble back into the church, I saw the dogs stop running and turn to their handlers. Instead of barking, they were snarling. Men shrieked and cried out. In the light of the beacon, I could see the Patrol was being torn apart by their own dogs.

This was the work of Hecate, our guardian mother. I felt myself begin to shake. An overwhelming wave of pain surged from my belly and at last I looked down to see my stomach gaping open, my trousers soaked in blood. I fell to my knees as I watched the men die. I was dying myself. At least I had lit the beacon and I could die in Hecate's place of worship.

My body lost all control but before my head could pound against stone something broke my fall. My eyelids fluttered open. At first I thought my vision had gone, seeing three faces instead of one, but then I knew who it was. She touched my tattoos and the triple moon pendant.

"You heard me," I whispered as my life began to slip away. It felt as if my skin was being peeled from my muscles. A layer of my being was being stripped away.

"I hear all your prayers," she said.

"You bitch!" a man shouted close by. My attacker. He was still alive. I grabbed Hecate's arm in panic. Her head whipped toward him and her eyes glowed hot white. Her skin scalded my hand.

"I'll have both of you!" he screamed.

In an instant he flew across the church, hitting the stone wall. From the darkness two hounds emerged with eyes glowing the same fierce white as hers.

"You dare enter my sanctuary? You dare try to harm me or my daughter?" she sneered.

He attempted to rise to his feet but his head bashed against stone. He screamed and his head jerked back again. His eyes rolled to the back of his skull as his entire body convulsed and hit the wall again and again until his skull cracked open. Blood oozed from broken flesh and bone.

Hecate's lips smiled at this sight. I could feel myself falling further into an abyss of oblivion. I touched her hand and surrendered to whatever came next.

"Wake up!" The voice sounded like I was underwater, It continued to echo as I slowly rose to the surface. I opened my eyes. Hecate still held me.

"Am I dead?" I croaked. Her face went from one to three. I tried to focus. But I noticed I no longer felt pain from the wound in my belly.

"You were. And now you are not."

My eyes strayed toward the dead man slumped against the wall. Blood covered his face and neck. "Why did you save me?"

"We have much to accomplish. You had to be spared."

"My goddess ..." Tears fell from my eyes.

"Do not thank me yet. We have a temple to build and a lighthouse to restore. You are now an anointed high priestess. A true disciple of Hecate."

It would be done. In Hecate's name, I would preserve her ways of the past with words, deeds and art. I would do it for her – and to inspire a new world for my sisters. A world of possibility and goddess magic.

Hecate – Torch of Witchcraft

Of all the goddesses in the Greek pantheon, Hecate is perhaps the one who most captures our attention today. She seems to be having a renaissance. Scroll through social media and you will find a plethora of prayers, oracle readings, pictures of altars and so on, posted by modern witches who are calling upon Hecate and integrating her various aspects into their lives. Her image and stories are important to modern witchcraft because she is the Greek goddess of sorcery, necromancy, witchcraft, phantoms, the moon and the night.

Her mythology, however, is elusive. She appears in the tales of many other gods and goddesses, yet has no definitive text of her own.

She appears in the 8th century BCE, in Hesiod's poem "Theogony" about the adventures of the Titans. She was born in Thrace, the daughter of the Titans Perses and Asteria. Zeus granted her dominion in both the heavenly and earthly realms. In the poem she is said to sit beside kings who faithfully worship her. She guides soldiers to victory in war, and guides athletes competing in games. Fishermen and hunters call to her to ask for her aid. However, she also has the power to take their success away.

In the "Hymn to Demeter" in the *Homeric Hymns*, we see Hecate's desire to help others in the myth of Persephone's abduction by her uncle Hades. When Persephone's mother, Demeter, searches the world in anguish for her lost daughter, Hecate aids her with flaming torches in hand. Together they visit Helios, the embodiment of the sun, who has the power to see all.

The 3rd-century BCE poet Theocritus shows us Hecate's magical side in "Idyll II The Sorceress". He calls her "the one who dwells in the shade" and says she is capable of working witcheries as potent as those of Circe or Medea. He also describes Hecate rituals taking place at crossroads.

The 1st-century Latin poet Virgil gives a vivid description of the offerings Aeneas makes to Hecate to gain entrance to Hades. A priestess takes four black cows and pours wine over their foreheads. She plucks hair from between their horns and tosses it into a bonfire. Then their throats are slit and their blood is collected into bowls. Aeneas then sacrifices a black lamb. They call upon Hecate to accept the gift.

As the sun begins to rise, Hecate answers. The ground beneath their feet moves as do the hills. Dogs howl in the distance. The keeper of the underworld is appeased.

Hecate is associated with the triple moon, torches, black hounds, polecats, snakes, keys and, when triple bodied, the crossroads (having three bodies gives her an advantage when facing a choice of different directions). The torches help others find their way. The triple moon represents the waxing, full and waning moons, which stand for the different seasons of womanhood – maiden, mother, crone. She is also associated with the stropholos, or the wheel of Hecate, a spiral maze with a five-pointed star in the centre. What is life if not a journey through a maze, with many twists and turns as times goes on? Hecate can be our trusted guide through the material world as well as the spiritual. With power over multiple realms and many attributes at her disposal, she is a formidable goddess to have on your side.

Hecate Wisdom

Whether or not you practise witchcraft, Hecate is a stunning portrayal of the many ways femininity manifests in magic. We all experience crossroads in our lives and have to go through our own dark nights of the soul. Hecate can be our torch when hope is dim. Sometimes we need just enough light to put one foot in front of the other until we get through the crisis. Her three faces remind us to pause, to see things from different perspectives and to consider alternative directions, especially if we're feeling stuck. Also, she reminds us that we do not have to remain in the same energy or patterns. We can choose to shift if we feel called to. Our personal power is magic, like this goddess.

Hecate shows us the light when life gets dark.

INDEX

Note: page numbers in **bold** refer to illustrations.

A

B

C

D

E

F

G

H

I

Q

R

S

T

U